T0125769

The Liberators

of Willow Run

MARIANNE K. MARTIN

Bywater BOOKS

Ann Arbor
2016

Bywater Books

Copyright © 2016 Marianne K. Martin

All rights reserved. No part of this book may be reproduced, stored in a retrieval system, or transmitted in any form or by any means, without prior permission in writing from the publisher.

Print ISBN: 978-1-61294-079-3

Bywater Books First Edition: October 2016

Printed in the United States of America on acid-free paper.

E-Book ISBN: 978-1-61294-080-9

By payment of the required fees, you have been granted the non-exclusive, non-transferable right to access and read the text of this e-book on-screen. No part of this text may be reproduced, transmitted, downloaded, decompiled, reverse engineered, or stored in or introduced into any information storage and retrieval system, in any form or by any means, whether electronic or mechanical, now known or hereinafter invented, without the express written permission of Bywater Books.

Cover designer: Ann McMan, TreeHouse Studio

Bywater Books
PO Box 3671
Ann Arbor MI 48106-3671
www.bywaterbooks.com

This novel is a work of fiction. All characters and events described by the author are fictitious. No resemblance to real persons, dead or alive, is intended.

Always for Jo

And for my mother, Vivian L. Martin, R.N.,
whose surgical nursing skills were outweighed only by
her compassion. During her years at the Crittenton
Home she gave "her girls" the love and respect and
empowerment that much of society denied them.
And she understood the blessings that sharing them
with her family meant to both. She stood strong for
what she believed was right and she taught me to do
the same. Her love and strength are sorely missed.

Acknowledgments

It's a solitary thing, writing is, tucked away in the private places of life. Alone with pencil and paper, with questions and research and plot lines in my head vying for justification on paper. Just me and the words.

Until it isn't. Until it's time for edits and jacket copy and cover art and marketing, and an essential team of women who help take my story from its scratched in longhand first breath of life to a finished product that I can be proud of and into the hands of readers. These are tasks that I am grateful to have in the hands of the incomparable team at Bywater Books. My thanks and gratitude to Editor-in-Chief Kelly Smith, editor Caroline Curtis, proofreader Nancy Squires, cover designer Ann McMan, publisher Salem West, and publicity director Rachel Spangler. Without you my words remain in solitude.

And without the original liberators, the Rosies of World War II, this story would not have been possible. Their personal stories of commitment and sacrifice chronicled a time of change and helped shape a new world of employment and independence for women. Their impact is immeasurable.

There are times in life when, although good friends are always appreciated, something happens that shows them to be blessings beyond measure. A recent accident and unexpected surgery has done just that. Thank yous are simply not enough. My Bywater family made sure that this book came out on time. And I do not know what I would have done without Marcy Tyson and Courtney Duke being there through the emergency and surgery and mornings and nights of care. Or what I would have done without Jan Payne and Sally Dawson taking me and the pups into their home to feed and care for us. You are all blessings without measure and I love you.

Chapter 1

We are engaged in a war on the successful outcome of which will depend the whole future of our country . . . We will win this war only as we produce and deliver our total American effort on the high seas and on the battle fronts. And that requires unrelenting, uninterrupted effort here on the home front.
Franklin D. Roosevelt, Fireside Chat, May 2, 1943

Nearly every word she had written was a lie. Audrey Draper folded the letter, slipped it into the envelope, and addressed it to her parents.

She wasn't staying with a friend's family, not anymore, and she wasn't pining for her guy in the service. Bradley Willis never stole her heart. There *was* no Bradley Willis. It was a lie, one of many. Audrey Draper had become a good liar.

The lights of Jack's Ford shone through the front window of her Willow Village apartment, and Audrey checked the clock beside the bed. 5:30. He was early this morning. Audrey scooped up her jacket and keys, snapped off the overhead light, and locked the door behind her. She returned Jack's smile and climbed into the back seat.

"Mornin', Lucy," she said as Jack's wife turned to greet her from the front seat.

"I'm sorry, Jack forgot to tell you yesterday that we'd be picking you up early now."

"No, that's alright. I was up early today."

Jack made eye contact in the rearview mirror. "I want to let Lucy off at the entrance on the other side of the plant from now on. Less of a walk for her."

"He worries too much," Lucy said. "This baby's not comin' any time soon."

"How long will they let you work?" Audrey asked.

"Until I tell them I can't. And I'll work as long as I can. We're gonna need every bit of that money once this little one is here. They're offering $300 if I go back to work within six weeks after birth."

Audrey nodded. Exactly. And at $5 an hour and nine hours a day, it was more money than they could make anywhere else. It was more money than Audrey's own father made back home.

"If they have any chance at all to meet their production goal, they can't afford to lose workers for any reason," Jack added. "The newspapers are calling us 'Will it Run,' and Truman's War Investigating Committee is sayin' we're nowhere near our projected numbers, so the plant's trying to increase the crew numbers. We have a new one to our crew comin' in today, and we're goin' on overtime starting this week." Jack stopped the car at the intersection and waited for traffic, most of which was also headed to the Willow Run bomber plant. He spoke as he waited his turn. "If Lucy weren't working in payroll, though, I'd be puttin' my foot down about how long she works. I don't care how much money we're talkin'."

Lucy turned to face Audrey again. "Did you see the government ad? *Can you use an electric mixer? If so, you can learn to operate a drill.*"

"They're tappin' the only well with water," Jack offered as he merged the car into the line of traffic.

Women. It made Audrey smile. That previously untapped well was supplying a workforce that had already exceeded all expectations. Smart, dedicated, and efficient. They didn't have to be on the front lines to help win this war. If the government needed bombers, then this plant was going to build more than any other in the country. And it would be the women who made it possible.

༺ ༺ ༺

She was there at the station waiting, with that expected wide-eyed look of anticipation, when Audrey and Jack arrived.

"I'm Nona," she said in an accent that clearly indicated that she was from deeper south than Ohio. "I finished training school Friday and Mr. Bentley assigned me to your crew."

2

"He must have been impressed, then," Audrey said, extending her hand. "You won't find a faster riveting crew on the floor."

"Hey, *if you can use a mixer* . . ." Jack said and grinned at Nona's puzzled look.

"The government ad," Audrey explained. "It may make us even more grateful for the training school."

"Is it true the President himself was here?" Nona asked.

Audrey nodded. "Last year. Jack here got to see him firsthand."

"President Roosevelt himself, as close as I am to you right now," Jack said and flashed a toothy smile. "Rode right down through the whole plant in the car with Mr. Ford. We got a lot to do to live up to them promises Mr. Ford made, but by God, we're gonna do it."

The last three members of the crew arrived with only enough time for a quick introduction and directions from Jack. "You make sure you follow safety rules," he directed at Nona. "You're rivetin' for Janice and I'll have none of *my* crew goin' down to negligence." He went over the rest of the safety rules despite her obvious compliance. "Head scarf, trousers, flat shoes, no jewelry?"

"Yes, sir."

"Okay, let's get at it, then."

The sound of Mac, the company's Star Man, bellowing "Will it run?" signaled the beginning of the shift. It was his angry response to the initial plant problems that had prompted the nickname. "You answer them sons-a-bitches with your numbers," he reminded them with the anger and determination that he used to drive the crews all day long. And their numbers were the only response he heard.

So the day began, with any talk past introduction waiting for the lunch break. And even then it was squeezed between bites and dotted with nods. It wasn't until the end of a long nine-hour shift that Audrey had a few uncompromised minutes to find out a little more about their new crew member.

Jack lacked her curiosity and went on ahead to walk Lucy to the car while Audrey and Nona walked at a more casual pace to the closest exit. It *was* curiosity, Audrey admitted, and not merely born of wanting to know who she was working long hours next to. And not because of a natural draw to women that had seemed always to have been there. It was true that Nona offered a smile that made you smile back without a single reason why. But she was also the first Negro Audrey had ever talked to. There were no Negroes in the neighborhood she grew up in, none in her school, or at her church. There was only the woman who walked from the bus stop once a week to clean the Bronson's house down the block, and the old man who picked up trash around Mr. Peter's grocery store. There never seemed to be any reason to talk to them—or a reason not to. And now there was Nona and an undeniable curiosity.

"You came up from Kentucky all by yourself?" Audrey asked. "Don't your parents worry?"

"There were articles in the papers every day about what we can do for the war effort and how much money can be made. Our papa said he doesn't know another place on this earth I could make this much. I want to go on to college and this is the only way I can do that."

"Where are you staying? I was so lucky to get into the Village. They're putting up housing as fast as they can build them. Outside of that, seems like you can't find a bed in a closet within twenty-five miles of the plant."

"Our church back home connected with a church in Detroit that lets workers stay in their basement. I take the plant bus back and forth. Far from the comforts of home, but it's worth it." They stopped at Audrey's exit. "The bus picks up at the other end," Nona said. "It seems like I'm walking a mile. I've never seen anything this huge in my life."

"There isn't anything else this huge in the world. Mr. Lindbergh himself calls it the Grand Canyon of the mechanized world. I'm really lucky that I can ride with Jack. I don't want to keep him waiting, Nona, so can we talk more tomorrow?"

"Oh, sure," Nona replied with a look of mild surprise. "Sure, I'd like that."

"So I'll see you in the morning. It's a six o'clock start time until they tell us different. Don't be late."

"I won't," Nona said. "You'll see. I'll never be late."

Audrey offered a smile. "Tomorrow then," she said and slipped out the door.

Jack was waiting and Audrey quickened her steps and jumped into the back seat. "I didn't mean to make you wait."

"Naw, just a couple of minutes," he replied.

"There are so many things I want to know about Nona. In a way I feel like Curious George straight out of my little cousin's storybook. Have you ever worked with a Negro, Jack?"

He took his turn and pulled into traffic. "Yeah, at the River Rouge Plant. Ford's been hirin' 'em as fast as he can get 'em up here from the South. Payin' big money, too."

"I noticed more hiring in here now, too," Lucy added. "A lot of people aren't too happy about it, though."

"Ah, they probably never worked with 'em before," Jack said. "Most of 'em never worked with women before, either. But for now, they're gonna have to get used to it. Everybody's gotta pull together, don't matter what color ya are or if you're a man or a woman. They need B-24s and, by God, we're gonna give 'em all they need. We're gonna win this war."

He believed that. Audrey was sure of it. A freak shop accident had taken his father's life, and he had no brothers. If he weren't the last male in the family, he'd be fighting this war as a soldier, not as a crew chief in a bomber plant. She saw that in him every day, pushing his crew to top efficiency, proud to build the best damn plane our pilots had ever flown, and expecting the same dedication from everyone else. He was a good man and she was proud to work with him.

"I'm bettin' on it, Jack. I'm bettin' we win this war right here from this plant."

Chapter 2

It seemed an imposing building the first time Ruth Evans saw it, sitting back off the road. Large, distant, brick. Before it a monotony of green—lawn mowed tight, shrubs trimmed and dutiful. No companions of color defining the edges, separating the boundaries. The Crittenton Home. There was no sign, the name had been mentioned only days before the trip, squeezed out tightly in her mother's terse tone, the words clipped short.

For seven hours, the entire drive from Bloomington, Indiana, her father had spoken only when they stopped for gas or for a bite to eat at a roadside diner. He focused—as if speaking was too distracting—on the road, on every bite of food, on lighting one cigarette after another until he had smoked two days' worth. He was more distant than her new home. Now, no matter how hard she tried, she would never gain her father's favor, and she could no longer be her mother's shining example of virtue and purity.

And it was never more clear than right now. Harold Evans lifted his daughter's suitcase from the trunk of the car, carried it to the front door, and left it. He returned to the car and slid into the driver's seat without a word.

Margaret stood facing her daughter outside the car. Her tone held no warmth, but her eyes seemed to plead. "If you would only marry him," she said.

Ruth dropped her focus, left the pleading to stare at the red-painted toenails peering from her mother's favorite open-toed heels. "But I don't—"

"It's too late for that to matter." Margaret's coolness turned terse.

"You should have thought of that before . . ." She looked away, across the drive to the hideaway she had chosen for the duration of her daughter's pregnancy. "Is there anything you want me to tell Paul?"

"No."

Her eyes came back, pleaded again. "Ruth."

"No, mother. Nothing." There was an urge, a need to tell her why, to make her hear the truth. It was a strong urge, a gathering of forces she had no name for that riled against her silence. The strength of her thoughts, of the feelings squeezed so tightly into submission, frightened her. What if they broke their bounds, spewed into the open? And who would suffer most from that kind of honesty? Paul? Her mother? Herself? Or, would she never recover from that self-destruction?

Her mother's tone changed, more motherly now than it had been in months. "They won't allow any contact while you're here. No visits or calls," she said as her eyes returned to her daughter's. "Even from us."

Ruth frowned. "Why?"

"They want to avoid any problems."

"Like what?"

The expression on her mother's face was one Ruth was quite familiar with—eyes evasive, brow smoothed of its frown, dismissive. "They will explain it all to you once you get settled."

Exactly what she had expected. Maybe it was time to stop challenging her mother to breach her discomfort and answer the many questions, some begging for answers since childhood. So many *whys* left to her own investigation, her own discovery. It was a challenge her mother did not understand. The only answers she offered were suggestions that some things are not discussed, and life is easier and happier when you accept what is expected of you. But as hard as her mother tried, lifting her voice to put an air of lightness to the subject, she was never convincing. Ruth had never been able to define it, what it was that betrayed her mother's conviction, but there was something that always made Ruth doubtful. She felt as if her mother was holding something too tightly, restraining it. What began as a guessing game had become a silent grasping that often made Ruth angry. Honesty simply was not possible.

And so she left it—no further challenge, no more discomfort for her mother. Ruth followed the woman who answered the door, turned to see the feeble attempt from her mother to smile, and let it go.

The woman introduced herself, Mrs. Stranton. The name suited her, Ruth decided. Maybe it was the dark hair streaked with silver pulled severely into a bun or the rod-straight posture, but somehow it fit her perfectly.

"Ruth, is it?" she said, leading the way up the stairs to the second floor. "That's a fine Biblical name. And we will be doing our best here to help you make the rest of your life worthy of it."

Worthy. The word stung—smarted as badly as her father's hand had across her backside. The physical sting had always disappeared by the end of the day, but even years hadn't taken away the emotional sting. It stayed with her, multiplied each time she disappointed her father, no matter how hard she tried to please him. And now, this time, she knew there would be no making up for *this* disappointment.

"You'll find the daily and weekly schedule there on top of the bureau," Mrs. Stranton explained as she ushered Ruth into the little room. "And the house rules are there, as well. You get settled in and one of the girls will be by in a bit to show you around." With a polite smile she closed the door behind her and left Ruth alone.

The only window looked out over the back of the property. A groundskeeper was mowing the area designated as a yard, a large rectangle carved into the surrounding overgrowth. No visible buildings, no neighbors, little chance of voyeurs into society's embarrassment.

Ruth stepped back from the window and placed her hand over the soon-to-be noticeable belly bump. An embarrassment. That's what she had become.

A knock on her door stopped her thoughts short of introspection, delayed the self-judgment for later. Her hostess's name was Susan, tall and pretty in an untouched, natural way. No lipstick or mascara, but a smile that offered instant warmth and gave Ruth the first sign that someone saw her and not merely her situation. And before she said a word, Susan relieved one big concern—the girls in the home were not all teenagers. Susan was a peer, someone she could relate to, someone who might be able to lessen the isolation, and temper the loneliness.

"Come on and I'll show you around," she said, as if she were about to show Ruth a grand hotel.

Ruth followed her hostess down the hallway of closed bedroom doors, down through the dining commons and the reading room and past open doors where classes were being held. The duty schedule was pointed out and a brief explanation of what she would be expected to do in the kitchen and laundry. Nothing, she found, beyond the duties she was used to taking care of at home, right down to ironing the sheets on the mangle ironer.

"I must tell you," Susan said, "there are consequences to not taking your turn on the duties schedule. Social privileges like playing games in the main room with the other girls would be denied." She turned to make eye contact. "And then you will have to go to remedial class."

"It's no more than I would be doing at home. Why wouldn't I take my turn?"

"I have the same responsibilities at home, too, but some of the girls either haven't learned what is expected or they refused their duties. If you ask me, all the classes here are remedial, but the staff are bound to make us all good girls before we leave here."

She flashed another big smile and all Ruth could think of was how easily Susan smiled, and how there didn't seem to be one reason warranting a smile at all. Wasn't she being hidden away to avoid the embarrassment—her own, her family's—letting them fabricate whatever lie might explain such a long absence? Wasn't she away at some out-of-state school, or taking care of an elderly relative?

Maybe Susan was simply happy that it was nearly over for her. Maybe she would be able to go back home, reputation intact, and start fresh. Maybe that was really possible.

Chapter 3

Nona was good to her promise, never late, always there early. And she was indeed fast, handling the rivet gun as well as anyone Audrey had seen. But she had a ways to go to make a believer out of old Mac, the Star Man. He was a gruff old shop rat with years of working in the Ford plant behind him. Supervising women was nowhere near the top of his "okay in his life" list. And having Negro women in the plant, well, it wasn't even *on* the list.

But his lack of eye contact, constant scrutiny, and grunts for replies didn't deter Nona. She said very little, smiled still, and riveted so accurately that Janice bucked as fast she ever had and backed out only two rivets in three weeks. Unless she decided to leave on her own, it looked as though Nona was here to stay.

It wasn't as easy to gauge how the rest of the crew felt about Nona. The interplay, or lack of it, captured all of Audrey's curiosity and filled those few free minutes hiding in even the most tightly scheduled day. It was amazing how much information could be gathered during a ten-minute break or a twenty-minute lunch.

Bennie never gave much more than smiles and nods, and he offered the same to Nona. And when he did manage more, Nona graciously listened for as long as it took for him to stutter through each sentence. Not one interruption, not one sentence finished for him. Tolerant and understanding, and a refreshing contrast to June the Oblivious.

"Did you sss-sss-ssee the ne-ne-new film?" Bennie asked. "That's ooouurr b-b-b-*bomber* they're flyin'."

Nona shook her head. "Where's it being shown?"

"All the theaters," June inserted, "right before the feature show. Bennie imagines he'd be flyin' one of our bombers if they'd let him in, not buildin' 'em."

Audrey shot her a hard look. "June," she said.

"Well, it's no disgrace to be 4F," June continued. "It's not like he's a dodger."

"*June*," Audrey said again.

"He is one fine riveter," June continued, as though he wasn't sitting three feet away. "I dare say he could beat any challenger."

Jack pushed back his chair and picked up his thermos. "Come on, Bennie," he said. "I got those pictures back I promised you."

Audrey caught Nona's eye as the men left the table. It didn't seem that she needed to say anything.

Undaunted, June chattered on. "You're coming out with us tonight," she directed at Audrey, "aren't you?"

"I'm exhausted," she replied.

"I don't care how tired I am," June continued. "I'm gonna cook with helium tonight. That's what Saturday nights are for, dancin' and forgetting about work and war and all the bad things that could happen. And there's no better way that I know of to put worry about our men out of our heads."

"I know," Audrey replied, aware that the invitation was meant for her and Janice, and not extended to Nona. "Good band music and dancing helps take your mind off everything, but . . ."

"Come on! Janice and them are all going." A nod from Janice. "Mother's got my boys overnight, so I got all night to cut a rug and have a few drinks with the girls. We've earned it. Right, Janice?"

Thick-boned and as strong as any bucker on the line, Janice never seemed to lack the energy to go out with the girls. "My Bobby don't mind. I write him a letter every night. He knows I'm workin' hard to help win the war. Are you worried that your Bradley won't understand and think you're goin' out on him?"

Audrey shook her head. "No, he trusts me. I'm just tired. Count me out tonight. I'm going to write letters, then get horizontal and listen to the radio."

෨ ෨ ෨

"I've never met anyone like you," Nona said, pulling off the headscarf and loosening flattened hair with her fingers.

"I can say the same thing about you," Audrey replied as they began their daily walk to the exit.

"You would have told June you'd go dancing tonight if I hadn't been sitting right there, wouldn't you?"

"Oh, I don't know. I'm pretty tired."

"Is that it?" Nona asked, then waited for Audrey to meet her gaze. "Or is it that June's insensitivity bothers you?"

Audrey smiled and pulled her eyes away.

"So tell me," Nona continued, "is she just insensitive, or is she sending a message to Bennie and me that she's only tolerating us because of the war effort?"

They stopped just outside the door. "I think I have June figured out," Audrey said. "But the answer to your question isn't a simple yes or no." She hesitated a moment and Nona made no indication of leaving.

Audrey's hesitation wasn't about whether to ask, but about how to make what she would ask possible. She still knew so little about her new friend—what life was like for her outside of work, what she enjoyed, what she hoped for.

"I'm starving," Audrey began. "Well, I'm always starving, but, is there some place where we can get something to eat and talk? I can tell Jack to go ahead and I can get a bus home later."

She couldn't identify what it was that she saw in Nona's eyes, or even what she expected to see. There wasn't an easy answer, that much she did know. And she knew Nona had to be the one to make the decision.

The space between Nona's brows pressed into a dark v-shaped crease. "It would be nice if we could. It seems like we should be able to, I know," she said.

"We can't, can we?"

"It would be very uncomfortable," Nona replied. "I can't go to white places, and it would be about as bad for you to come with me to a Negro place. There are too many people up from the South with a lot of mistrust. I wouldn't want to put you in that situation."

Audrey nodded. "I guess we have to decide if being friends is going to be worth trying to work around a lot of obstacles."

"It is to me."

"I'll tell Jack to go ahead. Let's get cart sandwiches and meet at the picnic table by the air-raid shelter."

ฅ ฅ ฅ

The wooden plank table sat outside the entrance to the shelter, underground firebrick-lined corridors stretching beneath the plant. If the war came to home soil, it stood to reason that it would be here in order to destroy America's largest war machine, and they would be ready. The Army, stationed on the east side of the airport, was there to protect the plant, the shelter was there to protect the workers.

Audrey placed the sandwiches on the table and settled across from Nona. The sounds of the plant were replaced by the not too distant sound of constant testing patterns and planes taking off and landing.

"Is it true," Nona began, "that Mr. Lindbergh himself helps test the planes?"

"Uh, huh," Audrey managed with a mouth full of sandwich.

"We *are* important here, aren't we? This plant, I mean."

Audrey swallowed and motioned toward the railed-off, square hole of the air-raid shelter near the parking lot. "Are you worried that we'll have to use that?"

Nona looked over her shoulder, then nodded. "I worry that the other Negro workers and I won't be allowed down there."

Audrey stopped short of her next bite. "I don't want to believe that that would ever happen." She watched Nona drop her eyes and say nothing. "I'm being naive, aren't I?"

Nona looked up and nodded. "But your heart is in the right place. I can't say that about everyone."

"Like Mac and June," Audrey said with a nod. "Mac doesn't like me much, either. *Nice* women don't wear trousers and work in plants. They don't make decisions for their family and they don't go out dancing while their men are fighting a war."

"So he's not pleased with June, either."

"No. She has children and has no business in a plant, or anywhere

14

outside her home. I'm convinced that he holds his tongue only because he knows the war effort needs women in the workforce."

"So that's *his* sacrifice," Nona replied, "having to work with women—and now a Negro woman."

"And they damn well better return to their 'place' when this war is over." Audrey motioned palm up with her hand. "Mac hates change, and the world has been turned on its end. He can handle rationing, coming out of retirement to work long hours and putting his money into war bonds, but . . ."

"Is there anything more I should do to avoid problems?"

"You're fine. I'm fine. Even June, oblivious as she is, is fine. We'll all be fine."

"Maybe you can be sure for yourself," Nona replied. "But you can't be sure for me. You see a couple of possible problems, the ones you bump shoulders with every day, but you don't see the ones around the next turn, waiting on the corner—people that judge the color of my skin and not my heart. You don't see them because you don't have to."

"Naive again. And I don't want to be, Nona. I sure can't be much of a friend that way."

"Please don't take this wrong. But why do you want to be my friend?"

Audrey finished the last bite of sandwich. Did she even know why herself? When had she ever thought consciously about why friendships started? Didn't they just happen? Growing up on the same block, sitting next to each other in class, working together. Common place, common interest, convenience. Attraction. It seemed that endings were more memorable than beginnings. And Nona?

"I left everything behind me," Audrey began, "my family and friends, my life there."

"I did, too."

"So," Audrey added, "do we need to know why?"

"Beyond that we are longing for someone to talk to, or that we're hoping to find someone who likes us for who we are, I suppose not. It would have been a lot easier, though, to be friends with someone like June. Someone you have a lot more in common with."

If Nona even knew how little in common they had. Audrey sipped her Coke while Nona finished her sandwich. A shared silence slowed their conversation and allowed a moment of thought. Important when you were tempted to say more than you should. Too much, too soon. Too much at all could be a big mistake.

"You asked me why," Audrey said, "and it's making me try to put words to thoughts that hadn't had them before. Some thoughts and feelings that never got talked about, so I'm not sure this will make a lot of sense."

"It will make more sense than me trying to read your mind."

"Sometimes *I* can't even read my own mind." Audrey added a grin. "But, here goes. First, you have to know that I was the kid in school who asked all the annoying questions like, why don't boys all have one color of eyes and girls all have another color? As far back as I can remember I have wanted to know more and see more than my little part of the world. I'm not a person who is satisfied with what I'm told or what is expected. I want to see for myself. I want to make my own decisions. I don't want to be trapped in June's world."

"There's no chance that I will be trapped in June's world, but since I am working with her, tell me about her world."

"I think right now it's a pretty scary place," Audrey said. "She's got two kids, her husband's piloting a Liberator for the Eighth Air Force, and she is having to work outside her home for the first time in her life."

"That's a lot of women right now."

Audrey nodded. "But for June, and a lot of women like her, this is only a moment in time. As soon as their husbands come home they will be able to go back to the life they're used to. And I try to understand that, even though it isn't what I want for my life."

"What *do* you want for your life?" Nona asked. "Don't you have someone serving, too? What will you do when he comes home?"

Try not to lie, Audrey reminded herself. Avoid, don't lie. "I always want to work. That way I will have my own money and I can make my own decisions. I love that I have my own space right now. It's just a little cold, apartment with cardboard-thin walls, but it's mine." Enough, she thought, stop right there. "How about you, what do you want your life to be like?"

Eyes distant and serious, Nona replied, "More than sleeping on the floor of a church." Then her face brightened. "I want to have enough money to afford more than two pair of shoes." She added a smile. "I have a plan for my life. I know exactly what I want, and that's to be an educator. I'm saving all the money I can, buying war bonds, and that way I will have enough to go to college when the war is over. I'm not going to do what my sister did and give up everything to get married. The man I marry will have to be educated, too. I don't think a man can respect a woman's goals unless he has those same goals."

The commitment in her tone, even tempered by the soft drawl of her accent, was convincing. This woman did indeed know what she wanted. She was believable, even inspiring. Grab your dream with both hands and don't let go. Find a way to overcome the obstacles— the restrictions, the attitudes. Something in Nona's eyes said that she would do just that.

"Does that surprise you?" Nona asked, with a slight tilt of her head.

It was Nona's question that surprised her. "No," Audrey replied, "it doesn't at all. You make me feel like a woman can do anything she sets her mind to."

"We can," Nona said, her eyes widening in possibility.

"We're proving *that* right here in this plant."

"I don't think even a few years ago people would believe we could do what we do every day. How can anyone deny now what we're capable of? Have you thought about what things will be like after the war?"

"Some things will never be the same for a lot of people. Families who lose someone in the war, women who enjoy their newfound independence, people who have moved to other parts of the country for work." Audrey replied. "I admit, though, that I don't have a solid plan for my future like you do. But the President is warning us that there is a lot of war yet to fight. We still have a high order and a lot more bombers to roll outta this place. I guess I'll have time to figure my future out."

"Having a plan in place can't hurt, Audrey. Think about it."

∽ ∽ ∽

Think about it—the future. Right. She'd done that once. Laid out plans, let the excitement color gray days and freshen stale air.

Audrey pushed her pillow into a wedge between the wall and the head of the narrow bed in the corner of her room. She settled back against the pillow, brought her knees up, and gave in. Just the thought of the love she had lost still quickened her heart and flooded all rational thought. Couldn't it have been, shouldn't it have been? The two of them had been so sure, so lost in the possibility. Obstacles to a life together, that life rendered powerless behind promises and laughter and an all-consuming passion.

Audrey rested her head against the wall and closed her eyes. There was no use trying to stop them. The memories boldly took their place, and Audrey tried to steel herself for the consequences. Her face was too clear, her blue eyes too compelling. Her smile, joyful and contagious, still pulled Audrey close, tempting her touch. Tender touches to delicate eyelids, soft cheeks, and warm lips. Even the thought brought back the promise in her murmurs, the sense of need in her kiss. They shared their need, shared a love hidden in stolen moments in an upstairs bedroom. Desire hushed into silent ecstasy. It was theirs alone. No one knew.

Audrey opened her eyes, trying not to see the change, not to see the love in Velma's eyes change to fear. It *was* theirs—until then.

She retrieved the letter from her mother from the nightstand, her only diversion until she could laugh at the silliness of Fibber McGee and Molly, and opened it. As much as she dreaded reading what she knew would be the usual questions and expectations too obviously formed into concerns, she longed for the familiar loops of her mother's longhand. Audrey held the stationery to her nose and breathed in the scent of her mother's favorite perfume. Evening in Paris. So fitting her mother, fashion-wise and beautiful. She had never doubted why her father fell so completely in love with her. She was perfect for him, smart in a way that made him smile, gracious in ways that made him proud. A woman who read *The New York Times,* listened to Edward R. Murrow and had no problem discussing foreign affairs, made a perfect partner to a well-respected Professor of European History. Yet, despite passing on the beauty of her high cheekbones and deep, dark eyes, she was a woman so unlike Audrey.

Outwardly, as Audrey had grown into her teen years, she and her mother had often been mistaken for sisters. But the similarities ended with the physical. She did not share her mother's love of fashion or fancy Betty Crocker recipes, or her dedication to reading long, dry books. And the biggest difference—unseen, unspoken, shared with only one other—was that Audrey could respect a man, but never desire one.

My Dearest Audrey,

Your father and I send our love and our hope that you are well. I must tell you that thinking of leaving your friend's family to live alone is quite worrisome to us.

A woman alone chances being robbed or accosted. And working in a factory, Audrey, is just not acceptable. I can't help but insist that you choose another way of giving to the war effort. If you had stayed at home you could have worked in the Victory Garden and helped me distribute the food to families.

I know a broken heart is not an easy thing to overcome, and although it is somewhat reassuring to know of Bradley, I wonder if you've given your heart away too quickly. You might better have waited and spent your time doing good for others.

Please stay where you are and as you write to Bradley, also select a name from the list I have included from your hometown and help make sure we are with our boys at every mail call.

I close with our love to you and a prayer that this war will be over soon so that we can all return to a good and normal life.

Your loving mother.

Chapter 4

It wasn't a pretty church, no old brick and stained glass claiming its dignified space like in the big Catholic churches. The One Way Tabernacle building was cement block, plain and simple, introduced by a hand-painted sign and a metal door opening directly to the city sidewalk. But its heart was its beauty—filled to overflowing with compassion and love. "There are no strangers here," Reverend Jennings was fond of saying. And in the time that Nona had spent there she had found that to be true, thankfully. They gave everything they had and asked for nothing in return.

The Reverend and the church elders had welcomed each of them off the buses, and when they ran out of homes for them to stay, they made the church basement as accommodating as they could. Rows of mattresses and blankets lined the floor on both sides of the clothesline draped with sheets to separate the women's space from the men's.

One bathroom for eleven women and virtually no privacy, but Nona was not complaining. There was nowhere near the amount of housing needed for the thousands of Southerners recruited to work in the war factories. To the Detroit and surrounding area factories, the Arsenal of Democracy, they were essential—but there weren't enough places for them to live, or places for them to eat, or transportation to work, or tolerance. The resulting stress had found its limit.

Negroes protested unfair conditions with a "bumping campaign." Dynamite, *Life* magazine called it, looking for a place to explode. Detonations had begun on Belle Isle and moved to Woodward Avenue, and soon hundreds were rioting.

The church was outside the most dangerous area, but Nona had blocks to walk to get to the bus to Willow Run. It was a small bus and whites boarded first. To be sure to get a seat, Nona needed to leave the church at 4:30 to be the first Negro there. She hurried along the sidewalk as the sun began inching back the shadows from the buildings lining her route. The Reverend's warning not to walk alone was well-meant, but Nona decided that wearing trousers and work shoes and moving quickly would have to be protection enough. Waiting for others and taking a chance on not getting on the bus was not an option. Being late to work could cost her job, a chance she was not willing to take.

She arrived at the stop as she did every day before anyone else and stood near the curb. About fifteen minutes later a young man arrived. Nona nodded a cordial greeting as he took his place in line behind her, then returned her attention to the street. Soon the white riders began to arrive and form a line a good ten feet away. Conversations began, muted, sporadic, mingling with an increase of motor noise and traffic.

Nona continued her watch in silence while the conversation from the white line grew louder. "Looks like some niggers took bumpin' up a notch," someone said loud enough for all to hear.

"They paid the devil for that out on Belle Isle," added another.

"Nah, it ain't been paid yet. Fightin's full-blown down Woodward. Still goin' since last night."

The young man waiting with Nona leaned forward and asked quietly, "What if the bus don't show up today? If the fightin's that bad . . ."

The thought hit sharply, turning Nona's head toward Woodward Avenue. Still no sign of a bus.

"I'm not waiting any longer," someone said, and left the white line.

Nona checked her watch. Already twenty minutes late. "Is there another bus that goes to Willow Run?" she asked the man behind her. He shrugged, and out of desperation Nona directed the same question to the woman at the head of the white line.

The woman started to answer, "I don't—"

"Why don't you niggers just go back to where you came from?" The man took a step from the line and added, "Nobody wants your kind here."

Whether it was to avoid an escalating confrontation or if it was just too long to wait for a now very late bus, a number of whites left the line and walked away.

Nona and the young man stayed, averting their attention to the street, and the comments lowered in volume and stayed among the remaining whites. Another look at her watch and it was clear that even if she could get on a bus right now Nona was going to be late. Something resembling panic grabbed at her, threatening the control she counted on and the belief she had in herself to make her plan work. She had been so sure.

She took a deep breath to calm the thumping in her chest. What now? She turned to find that there was no one left waiting except the young man and herself.

"They were right," he said, "ain't gonna be no bus today."

"I can't lose this job," Nona replied. "Maybe it's just late, and had to take a different route around the fighting."

"If they did that, they ain't comin' back for us," he said. "The whites got an excuse 'cause the bus didn't show. You and me can kiss that job good-bye." He turned to leave, then offered, "I'm gonna see if I can get into a plant closer."

☙ ☙ ☙

There are things that, over time, don't need conscious thought. They are givens, like FDR's Fireside Chats, and a card from her aunt arriving on the very day of Audrey's birthday every year. Nona's smile, greeting them in the morning had become a given, expected, taken for granted. So when Nona wasn't there to greet them this morning, Audrey became concerned immediately.

"Something's wrong," she said to Jack. "I'm going to check the bathroom. Maybe she's sick."

She wasn't in the bathroom, or in the tool room, or anywhere in sight. And when Audrey returned to their station Jack, was waiting with Mac.

"You find her?" Jack asked.

"No," Audrey replied, "but something must have happened. She's always the first one here."

"Yeah," Mac growled, "what happened is that she ain't here. They quit when they find it ain't like doin' a little laundry and cookin' dinner."

"That's not it," Audrey insisted. "I'd bet my next paycheck on it."

"Hey, Mac," Jack interjected, "if she's just late, we'll work through break to make up time."

"She's got 'til I get someone from graveyard to work overtime. Should take me ten minutes, so plan on working through that break anyway." He turned and bellowed over his shoulder, "We *will* make this run, goddammit."

There was never a problem getting someone to work overtime hours or even double shifts; the money was good and the cause pressed into the fabric of American daily life. Short of the ten minutes, a man about Audrey's father's age nodded to Janice, took his place, and started riveting.

Audrey bucked for Jack like any other day, two taps to let him know the rivet seated and she had smoothed over the ends. But her thoughts were far from usual. *Naivety. Her own very clear naivety.* That's where her thoughts were—about Nona, about herself, about women. What if it had been Jack and the car hadn't started, or Bennie who hadn't shown up? Would there have been questions—*what happened, is he okay, should we call someone and check?* What if it had been no fault of their own, would it have been overlooked and things gone on as normal? Could Nona expect the same?

Yes, it was becoming quite clear. Leaving the restrictions and expectations of parents, and even claiming those traditions were irrelevant for your own life, didn't mean they wouldn't still affect it. There was no running from them. She would always be standing nose to nose, challenging them, just like Nona.

෨ ෨ ෨

Nona held her spot near the curb for a moment, undecided, trying to hang on to the hope that the young man was wrong. "They need us," she said to herself. She wanted to believe that, to believe that being good at what you did, being on time every day, giving everything they asked for would protect her from something that wasn't her fault. But, there was no way to get there now, even late. She turned to walk back to the church.

As she did, an older Ford rolled to a stop against the curb just ahead of her. The driver swung open his door and popped his head up over the roof.

"Hey," he called, "were you waitin' on the bus?"

"Yes, the Willow Run bus," she replied. "Is it still coming? Did you see it?"

"Stopped up there in that mess on Woodward. They all left it, 'fraid it'll get burned like the cars."

"Thank you," she said with a nod.

"Hey, now," he said, "if you got some money for gas, I'll give you a ride." He pointed to the green B sticker, designating war worker on the windshield. "I'm workin' night shift at Rouge."

Nona hesitated.

"I help get people to work during my off time. Helps them out and gives me a little more spendin' cash."

"Yes," she replied. "Oh, yes, thank you." That he was using his rationed gas to help others out made her sure that she was making the right decision. And maybe, just maybe, getting to work, no matter how late, would save her job.

Nona settled into the front seat. She smiled at the man, and quickly realized that he was waiting for some money before starting out. She opened her purse as she did the math in her head. Thirty-five miles, fifteen cents a gallon. $5.25. Plus $3 for being so kind. She handed him the money and watched him count it.

His eyes went to her purse before she thought to close it. That's when it hit her, the second that her thought went from relief to fear. Before she could make herself reach for the door handle he said, "Could you spare a bit more?" His voice was requesting, asking, not demanding, and the look in his eyes matched his voice. Nona gave him her last dollar and fifty cents.

"That's all I have," she said.

"Thank you," he replied. He pulled away from the curb, and added, "Don't mind at all gettin' a ways away from Woodward."

"So it's really bad."

He nodded. "Cops aren't even tryin' to stop it."

"How's that going to help anything?"

He just shook his head and kept his eyes on the road. As he made the turn toward M-112, he added, "All I know is that we gotta watch out for ourselves, ain't nobody else gonna do it."

The miles rolled along in a comfortable silence. Easy when you didn't know someone. Fall into thought and let the landscape pass by without notice. He was right. Of course he was. It didn't matter where you were from Delaware: Des Moines, or Detroit. People would see what they wanted to see, believe what they grew up believing. Who she was beyond that they wouldn't know, or care to find out.

Nona looked at her watch. It was all she could do, watch out for herself and hope to save her job.

"Can't do no more than the victory limit," he said, noticing. "I go over thirty-five and get caught, they ain't givin' just a ticket now."

"No," Nona replied, "I don't expect you to speed. I'm truly grateful for your help." He was doing all he could, and without his help she wouldn't even have this slim chance. And it was that slim chance making her heart pound harder by the second. She fought the impulse to keep checking the time. The urge was relentless despite her doubt that minutes here or there would have any bearing on her fate. She was late—the rule and the promise broken.

And now? The fear of "what next" was real. She felt it now, over her anxiousness, drowning that slip of unrealistic hope. Yet, the moment the car stopped at the first plant entrance, Nona's only thought was to get to her post as fast as she could.

"Thank you," she said in a rush. "Thank you." She turned, clasped her purse tightly against the side of her breast, and broke into a full sprint. Across the parking lot, down nearly the length of the building, farther and faster than she had run since childhood games of tag.

"I'll explain," the words hard puffs from each pounding stride. "I'll explain." Her breathing heavy and heart thudding in her ears, Nona closed the remaining yards to the door. She rushed in, greeted by the deafening sound of all stations in full operation, dodged the cart in the aisle, and hurried on to the tool room. There she grabbed an apron filled with rivets and a rivet gun, and made her way to her station.

She stopped in the aisle short of the station. The crew was working at full capacity, a man she didn't recognize filling her position for Janice. What had she expected? Or was it just an unrealistic hope? One her logic should have squashed when the bus didn't show?

Mac was down the line hovering over another crew. Nona checked her watch. Her first chance to talk with someone would be the next ten-minute break. Anxious and trying to hang on to hope, she left to wait at the break table.

໑ ໑ ໑

Audrey saw her first, waiting at the table, apron and headscarf on and ready for work, rivet gun on the table. "Nona," she called, rushing to her, "what happened?"

"There are riots down Woodward," Nona replied. "There was no bus this morning."

Jack caught up, then immediately headed down the line to talk to Mac. Audrey could tell from his posture, pulled back and dismissive, that Mac was less than receptive. Jack's face said it all before he reached the table.

"He doesn't even want to know why you were late, Nona," he said.

"I lost my job then?"

Jack nodded.

"He won't even let her explain?" Audrey asked. "That's not right, Jack. The bus didn't show, and she still did what she could to get here as fast as she could."

"Maybe if I could talk to him," Nona said, "and explain how much this job means to me. Maybe—"

"He won't talk to you," Jack said with a shake of his head. "I know that for sure."

"But he'll talk to you," Audrey said. "Will you try, Jack? Please. You know how hard she works, how good a riveter she is." She met his eyes, trusted what she saw there. "She's like me, Jack, making our own way, no one watching after us."

27

Jack looked from Audrey to Nona. He didn't say anything, but motioned to Janice, coming back from the bathroom, to follow him. They stood a few yards away for a few minutes and then Jack headed back in Mac's direction.

Janice came back full of questions—*why are you late, how did you get here, are you back to work now*—and Nona was busy answering them. But Audrey kept her eyes on Jack.

At first his body language was typical Jack, hands in his back pockets, looking off to the side as he spoke. Mac was Mac, stoic and stiff, arms folded across his chest. Nothing to indicate movement in attitude or decision.

But when Mac raised a dismissive hand and turned away, Jack made a perfect Leo Durocher move, circling in front of him, tilting his head under a hard stare, going to bat for his player like any good manager would. Just what Audrey's gut would have her do if she could. She looked to see that both Nona and Janice, too, were fixed on watching Jack. Nona must feel the same thing in her gut—to plead her case, to talk to Mac herself. She would have pleaded it well. Who knew best what happened? Who best to explain, to promise, to convince of her intent, her loyalty? But she wasn't allowed that chance.

And what if it had been Audrey? *Would* it have been Audrey? If so, she would have wanted her chance. She would have been jumping inside even more than now, anxious to control her own fate. That same feeling she had before, jumpy and anxious, the day she made the decision to go away—to leave behind what she knew to embrace the unknown. And this was one of those unknowns. At least it was before today.

Jack was on his way back. He approached the waiting women. "Break's over," he said without expression. The women waited for a decision. "Nona," he said, looking right at her, "you're in."

Nona closed her eyes in relief before saying, "*Yes*, sir. Thank you."

Janice smiled and grabbed Nona's arm. "Come on," she said. "We have some catch-up to do."

"How did you do it?" Audrey asked, catching Jack's eye. "What did you say?"

"The truth." He offered a crooked smile and added, "And I gave him my best Leo the Lip. Look," he said, "it *was* a bad call. I don't care if she's a woman. I wouldn't care if she was purple. The fact is she's a helluva riveter and I'm damn proud that this crew is setting the production speed that other crews are bustin' butt to match. If Mac wants this plant to meet the production numbers expected, he'd be stupid to fire her."

"We were slow this morning, weren't we?"

"Like a beginning crew," he replied. "Janice said she was one-tapping him to push harder all morning. He couldn't seat 'em consistently and he had to back out a half a dozen. Yeah, we were slow." He put his hand on Audrey's shoulder. "So let's go kick up some dust."

∽ ∽ ∽

And raise dust they did. They worked out of pride and with something to prove. They worked straight through lunch and took only a few minutes' break for the mandatory salt tablets and water. They had a mission and they took hold of it with a singular determination.

Mac walked the line of crews, barking his version of encouragement over the sounds of rivet guns and drills and overhead tracks. "This ain't an afternoon stroll. Move it! You bakin' cupcakes or buildin' a bomber?" But for Jack's crew the harassment was even more unnecessary than usual.

They worked with precision, ignored hunger rumbling in their stomachs and muscles aching with exhaustion. By the shift's end six finished sections had been lifted and sent screaming along the overhead rail to installation. They had made a point, proved their case. A new standard set even after a slow morning. Mac didn't say a word, but it didn't matter.

The crew gathered at the exit, congratulating themselves and thanking Jack. Their celebration would be limited to that and a few backslaps. Jack wanted to get Lucy home, June had no sitter for the evening, and Nona couldn't be included wherever they went. So this would have to do.

"Thank you, everyone," Nona said as their little group dispersed.

"Wait," Audrey said, turning around. "What if you can't get the bus again tomorrow? What if the riots haven't stopped?"

Jack had stopped and turned as well. "What we did today won't mean shit to Mac if you're not here on time tomorrow," he said. "Leo the Lip got lucky today."

Nona hesitated. There hadn't been a spare moment to give serious thought to tomorrow. "I . . ." she began. "Maybe the Reverend at the church where I'm staying could spare the gas."

"I know," Audrey said, "You stay with me until we know the riots have stopped." She turned quickly to Jack, but didn't have to ask.

"It ain't the ride you got to worry about," he said. "It's not gettin' thrown outta your place, Audrey."

"No," Nona said with a shake of her head. "I won't let you take that chance."

But Audrey pressed on. "We'll make sure no one is watching tonight, and it's dark when we leave in the morning. It might only be one night."

Jack cocked his head. "I'll tell you one thing, if I ever get caught in a hole, you're the one I want on the other end of the rope."

Audrey smiled. "Then it's settled."

Chapter 5

For several months Ruth had watched as woman after woman made her decision. Some agonized openly, sharing their fears and their regrets, some struggled privately. Most of them in the end decided to give their baby up. The few that kept them were going home to marry the father and fight the stigma together.

The classes were supposed to help, lectures really, defining how proper young women conducted themselves, explaining the consequences of an errant image. It wasn't nice, you didn't want to be *that* young woman. And most agreed, at least outwardly. What they thought alone at night was anyone's guess.

Ruth was careful with her own honesty. She held it tightly, shared only pieces of it, and only with a woman she had grown to trust. Lillian Barton, proving to be far more than a wonderful RN, had passed the test. Those little tidbits of personal information commonly shared by others hadn't resurfaced through any of the expected sources. Mrs. Barton had kept them to herself. What Ruth needed even more than the ABCs of childbirth was someone to talk to. And being last on the examining room schedule offered the perfect opportunity to talk with Mrs. Barton every other week.

"Not one single thing to worry about," Mrs. Barton was saying as Ruth finished buttoning the oversized blouse. "You and the baby are coming along just as nature intended. You're doing beautifully."

"I think nature must intend this child to be an athlete of some kind," Ruth said, placing her hands on her belly. "I'm about worn out by the end of the day with all the antics in here. Do you think that means it's a boy?"

The nurse hesitated. There'd be no breach of the rule, no encouraging an attachment to a baby who would most likely be given away. "Have you thought more about what we talked about?"

Ruth nodded. Of course she had, every waking moment, trying to envision the future, fearing it, fearing the wrong decision. And her nights, filled with semi-conscious visions of a frantic search for a lost child.

"Do you want to talk more about it?" Mrs. Barton asked.

She tried not to sound desperate. "Yes," she replied, reminding herself that Mrs. Barton understood desperation. "I'm afraid of making the wrong decision."

"It's been cleared by administration for you to spend Sunday with us. My girls will help me get most of the dinner ready the night before, so it will be easy to serve on Sunday. That way Robert can pick you up about nine and the girls can get visiting with you out of their systems, and we will have plenty of time to talk after dinner." She put her arm around Ruth's shoulders. "This is your decision, Ruth, not the administration's, or your parents', or mine. You can decide what is best for you and for the baby, and I will be right here with you whatever you decide. Okay?"

"Is it this difficult for everyone?"

"I think it probably is for most. For some it seems it's easier for them to let someone else make the decision, but there must be times later when they wonder."

"How am I going to know if I made the right choice? Will *I* always wonder?"

"Wonder is natural, Ruth. We all wonder. What if we had married our high school sweetheart, or waited to start a family, or not waited? What if we had followed our dream for a career, or moved to another country? People wonder about all kinds of choices in their lives. What we want to avoid, if we can, are regrets."

"If I couldn't talk to you about this, I don't know—"

"But you can. As often as you want. I promise you that."

෨ ෨ ෨

Ruth expected no different. In the time that she had known Lillian Barton there hadn't been one time when she was unavailable, not one time when answering Ruth's questions seemed to be a bother, and *never* an air or judgment. Knowing she was there, was the one thing that kept Ruth strong, that gave her the confidence to question the expected. There was no one else who allowed or encouraged what it took to face the doubts and the fears, and what it would take to face the consequences of the decision she must make.

Spending a holiday, or a birthday, or just an occasional Sunday with the Bartons wasn't a new occurrence, nor was it exclusive to Ruth. It was an open invitation, approved regularly by the administration and accepted by many of the girls for as long as Lillian had been at the Crittenton. Everyone seemed to understand how important the sense of family was, especially during holidays, and so it was allowed and embraced.

Sometimes the day was shared by two or three of the girls. Today, though, it was exclusively Ruth's.

Lillian's daughters chattered on during dinner, completely at ease sharing their home and their teenage lives. Animated, talkative, and thirteen, Katie spent more time talking than she did eating.

"I just finished reading *The Clue in the Jewel Box* yesterday, and I think it was the best yet. I really do. I just love Nancy Drew, she is the smartest girl ever. Caroline still thinks Frank Hardy is smarter, but—"

"I do not." Being one year older did not afford Caroline much clout.

"You like him better because he's a boy."

"I never said that."

"Well, Nancy Drew would be my best friend if she was real, and we would solve all kinds of mysteries together and help people out."

Lillian smiled and leaned toward Ruth. "She will talk above eating, sleeping—"

"But not reading," Ruth added, and returned the smile.

"Maybe you should let Ruth enjoy her dinner, Katie," Robert suggested, "and eat your own before it's cold."

Katie took a quick bite and Caroline took advantage of her chance. "I've read all the *Hardy Boys* books, and *Nancy Drew*, too," she said. "But my favorite character is Jo from *Little Women*. Have you read that book, Ruth?"

Ruth nodded. "I have, and I believe she is my favorite, too."

"Don't you just want to know everything about—"

"It's such an old story," Katie interrupted. "Nancy Drew is about the world today. Don't you read Nancy Drew, Ruth?"

"I admit I haven't," Ruth replied. "What one do you think I should read first?"

"The first one, of course. I'll get it for you after dinner and you can take it with you."

"And now," Lillian said, "you need to be fair and let Caroline finish talking with Ruth, too. That is, if Ruth doesn't mind trying to talk between bites."

"Not at all," Ruth replied. "I enjoy this more than you know."

And more than Ruth could explain. Things were quite different around the Evans family table. She and her brother spoke only when spoken to, and there was no rambling on or bantering to disrupt the natural flow of dinner. Life in general was like that during her growing-up years—orderly, predictable. The rules were clear and, for the most part, followed. Roles, too, were clearly marked and followed. Her father's work supported the family and set their status in the community, and his was the last word on family decisions. Her mother's responsibilities were to manage the household, raise their children in their respective roles, and to keep her husband happy. It all fit together, worked like well-oiled social gears, just as it was supposed to—until someone stepped outside the lines and threw the gears out of synch.

The table had been cleared and the girls were washing up the dishes. Robert excused himself to read the war updates in the newspaper and left Ruth and his wife to their private talk.

"Thank you for a lovely dinner," Ruth began. "And I know I've told you this before, but you sharing your family with me means more than I can tell you."

"They are pretty special," Lillian replied, "and they don't mind being shared at all."

Special indeed. A man who, without judgment, allows his teenage girls to spend any amount of time with someone in Ruth's situation was refreshingly unorthodox. A tribute, Ruth decided, to Lillian's fine choice in men.

"You and your husband are raising two nice young women. And I'm sure it has been no easy task with you both working."

Lillian smiled and settled her shoulder into the back of the couch to face Ruth, sitting next to her. "They are alike in many ways, and different in so many others. It has been a challenge at times. I'm sure there are times when Robert wishes we were raising boys. But I don't know if I could bear sending sons off to war."

"My father seems quite proud to have my brother serving. I don't know how my mother feels. She adds to my father's proud rhetoric, but something in her expression doesn't match her tone."

"She's never talked to you about it?"

"Sometimes it seems like she says what she thinks she should," Ruth said. "I'm never sure."

"So it's more than a discussion about you being pregnant that's been missing."

Ruth released an audible sigh and nodded. "Discussions are not appropriate between parents and children. Children can ask questions and they will be answered, but . . ." The furrow between her brows softened and disappeared. "That's why I love how your girls talk *with* you. You have conversations with them. I've never been allowed that."

"I want my girls to come to me. I'm hoping that if they come to me now with silly things, they'll come to me with the big things later. I hope they will trust my advice enough to seek it out, and not think that they have to struggle with it on their own."

"What if they don't take your advice?"

"Would I love them any less?" Lillian slowly shook her head. "Worry about them, yes. And hope that their instincts about what will make their lives happy are better than the advice I offered. Beyond that, all I can do is make sure that they know I love them."

Ruth watched Lillian's face as she spoke—the gentle movement of her eyes, deep with sincerity, the lift of her cheeks, the promise of a smile to come. She tilted her head, a slight easy angle that seemed to *offer* her words, lay them in the place between them, a gift for Ruth to accept or not.

"I wish I could say that about my own parents."

"Maybe they just don't know how to tell you that they do still love you."

Ruth shook her head. "I'm an embarrassment. I'm afraid I will always see that in their eyes."

"They'll get past this, Ruth. Give them time."

"There's only one decision they would be okay with—if I kept the baby and married Paul."

"And you are sure that you don't want to do that?"

Ruth nodded. "Yes, I'm sure—about not marrying Paul, that is." As sure as anything she knew about herself. Sure for reasons she couldn't even tell Lillian. Not even someone with the empathy and understanding of Lillian Barton would be expected to understand why. And Ruth wouldn't expect her to try.

"Is that your decision or his?"

"Altogether mine. He would have married me before he enlisted if I had said yes."

"Does he know about the baby?"

Ruth frowned. "I wish I could be sure that he doesn't. It would make things less complicated. But I'm afraid my mother welcomes that complication."

"You think she has told him?"

"Even after I've told her not to, more than once. I can't trust that she hasn't. She thinks she knows what is best for me, for him, for everyone."

"It's a mother's affliction," Lillian said and smiled. "I think we all struggle with letting go of that control, some more successfully than others. The important thing is you knowing what is best for you. It should be your decision."

"Well, that one is made."

"And when you go back home, will—"

"I can't go back home."

"Why, Ruth?"

"I can't be the person my family wants me to be." Or Paul, or anyone, even Lillian. As compassionate and fine a person as she was, even Lillian would not understand the real Ruth. No one would.

"It's not unusual," Lillian was saying, "to feel like that. A lot of girls feel that they have let their families down. It seems that way because people are uncomfortable around unwed mothers. The made-up stories and separation, and living with lies to avoid embarrassment. It's no wonder you feel like you do." Lillian reached over and ran her hand down Ruth's arm to cover her hand. "I wish I could change that for you. I wish I could change a lot of things."

"I do, too."

Lillian gently squeezed Ruth's hand and released it. "Give your family a chance. It'll take time."

"I don't know if I can," she replied. Not entirely the truth. She did know that she couldn't, wouldn't, because she knew nothing would change. The time for believing, hoping that that would happen was over. She had tried, and failed. And despite the questioning she saw in Lillian's eyes, it wasn't something she could explain.

"Where will you go if you don't go back home? Do you have relatives you could stay with?"

"None who wouldn't expect the same from me as my parents do. I've been thinking about this for months now." Oh, much longer than that, if she were totally honest. But the decision had become so complicated. "I need to start fresh somewhere," Ruth continued, "on my own." She moved her hand slowly over her belly. "That's what makes this decision so difficult."

Chapter 6

Ruth settled into the chair next to Susan in a room filled with girl chatter. At twenty-five they were the old women in the room, and had become natural magnets for the youngest among them. Amelia, fourteen, slipped quietly into the seat on the other side of Susan and offered a shy smile. It was a smile that hid what she had told them only after weeks of building trust. And what she trusted them with stirred an anger in Ruth that she hadn't expected. How could there be no justice to punish a boy for taking advantage of such a young girl? Why would she be held accountable and not him? Here she was, isolated from support, from understanding, bearing the imposed guilt alone, and forced to listen to daily insults to her goodness.

The hum of chatter quieted as Mrs. Stranton entered the room. Spiral notebooks were dutifully opened and eyes directed at the woman guiding them to be better women. This week's lessons had already covered organizing the kitchen, the most efficient laundry methods, and nutritious dinner recipes. All essential to their role in the world and their self-respect as women. But Thursdays offered those not-so-subtle messages, tucked in among the *Improve Your Home Management* lessons, of how to get it right the next time. Obviously every girl in the room had gotten it terribly wrong, and it was Mrs. Stranton's mission to save this room full of wayward girls.

"For you girls who have reached your twenties," she was saying, "it is fine to accept a dinner invitation at a bachelor's apartment, but you must balance his attention between the meal and talking about matters that are of interest to him. And you must leave for home by ten o'clock."

Ruth's notebook was open, her pencil moving deceptively on the page. But it wasn't Mrs. Stranton's advice leaving its mark, it was her face. It somehow had more of an impact than her words. Susan noticed what she was doing as Ruth sketched the outline and roughed in the features.

Over the past months Susan had watched many of Ruth's sketches come to life—the squirrel visiting the feeder in the back yard, the doe that had gradually ventured closer as the girls sat quietly in the sunshine, Janie and her baby boy before they left to join her new husband, and recently Amelia. Their young friend was a study in contradiction—the soft, full cheeks dusted in pink, eyes wide and direct and sparkling with youthful innocence countered by the swell of pregnancy. Images captured before their next blink, caught in the updraft just before exhale.

Ruth often shared her sketch times with Susan, she welcomed the compliments and the encouragement. Wasn't there a career for her where her talents would be rewarded? Wouldn't there be many who would love a portrait of a loved one, or a company that could use her skills in advertising? No one had ever wondered that for her, or if they had they had never voiced it. It made her feel special.

So Susan watched as the shading set the highs and lows of the contours of Mrs. Stranton's face. Wide, high cheekbones and deep-set eyes, thin lips defined in bright red.

↬ ↬ ↬

"Lack of restraint," she was saying, "is exactly the thing that spreads disease and drastically weakens morale."

Ruth's pencil began feathering tentative lines in the dark hairline.

Mrs. Stranton continued. "Ultimately lack of restraint breaks down the moral health of the nation."

Ruth's pencil continued working in the hairline.

"And we must, each and every one, especially in this time of war, do our utmost to keep our nation strong."

Susan grasped Ruth's drawing hand and stopped its progress. Ruth could feel the quivering against her shoulder as Susan stifled her laughter at the horns emerging from Mrs. Stranton's hair.

"Remember, a man will respect you as much as you respect yourself. Let that be your daily reminder."

Head lowered, lips pursed, Ruth closed her notebook and waited for Mrs. Stranton to exit the room. As the other girls resumed their conversations and made their way to the door, Amelia leaned forward and asked, "What are you two laughing about?"

Susan snatched the notebook from Ruth's lap, flipped it open, and showed it to Amelia. "Oh," the girl said, quickly covering a rarely seen smile with her hand.

They were the last in the room, huddled together in giggles. "Well, shame on us," Ruth said, reaching across Susan and snatching back her notebook. "I'm sure the lack of restraint in this room alone has lost the war for us all."

Ruth read the look on Amelia's face before she heard the words. "You don't mean that," Amelia said, "do you?"

Susan put a reassuring arm around Amelia's shoulders.

"No, no," Ruth replied, "of course not. No one in this building, no amount of pregnancies in this country makes one bit of difference in this war. And *restraint* . . ." she stopped short of venting a rage that had been building since Amelia had confided in them. The sketch had only touched it, teased it, lightened it enough to allow just a glimpse at it. But there was so much more she wanted to say, needed to say for Amelia.

Ruth pulled her chair around to face Susan and Amelia. She directed her words, calm and measured, at Amelia. "No one has the right to include you in any lecture about restraint. No one. Not Mrs. Stranton, who doesn't know anything about you, and not your parents, who *should* know you. You've done nothing wrong, nothing to be ashamed of. The people who should be ashamed are the ones who have taken advantage of you and who have not protected or believed you. There is where the shame lies, not with you." Amelia's eyes never left Ruth's. "You have to believe that, Amelia. Believe it for yourself. Don't depend on anyone else believing it or even someone like me or Susan telling you to believe it." And then the words she had held, the ones that pushed and tested her own restraint. "You should not be ashamed, Amelia. You should be angry, very angry."

41

"Amelia," the voice from the doorway broke their huddle. "There you are. Your kitchen duty started ten minutes ago."

Without a word, Amelia rose and scurried from the room.

"You know," Ruth began, "I admit I'm nervous, even a little scared about having a baby, making the right decisions, what I'm going to do after. But, I can't imagine how scared that little girl is."

"You know what worries me most?" Susan asked. "That her parents don't believe her about the boy forcing her. Why wouldn't they believe her?"

"What if the boy won't leave her alone when she goes back home?"

"And her parents still won't believe her," Susan added. "If I were Amelia that would scare me more than anything."

"We need to know. We need to keep talking to her, and figure out how we can help."

Susan frowned and shrugged her shoulders. "You and I will be out of here before she delivers. What can we do when we'll be in three different states?"

"Maybe I can work something out with Nurse Barton," Ruth said. "I trust her. Amelia needs to trust her. I know I won't be able to come back here once I've left, but maybe there's a way I can stay in contact with Amelia until she delivers."

"And after that?"

"One thing at a time. I don't know exactly where I will be, but it'll be somewhere close by. I'm not going back home." The look she received was expected. The decision was one that Susan didn't anticipate.

"Why, Ruth? What will you do?"

"It's . . . it's not something I can explain. I'm just not going to be able to do what you will do. I'm not going to marry a boyfriend when he comes home and start my life all over. I'll start over, but somewhere else, alone."

"I think that would be even more scary than being shipped off to a place like this. At least this is temporary. I'll be going back to people I know, and I know where my life is headed from here. Doesn't the unknown frighten you?"

"Surprisingly," Ruth replied, "not as much as the known does."

Chapter 7

It didn't matter whether they had been friends or lovers, Audrey's choices always seemed to be fraught with difficulties. Sarah wasn't close enough in age to satisfy her mother, Judith wasn't feminine enough to be acceptable, Mary appeared much too close for everyone's comfort, and Velma, well, she was invisible. The realization wasn't new, just shined up and brighter tonight. And no matter who came into her life there seemed little chance of the rules changing.

So, naturally, in this new place with her new life, she had a friendship neither race would accept and a guarantee that if she were to fall in love again it would have to be a tightly held secret. Secrets and lies. Not something she wanted to think about tonight.

They sat at the little table against the wall across the room from the bed. "I think this is the best tuna salad I've ever had," Nona said, lifting the last forkful.

"It's the goat cheese. Who would've ever thought they'd make cheese out of goat milk, and that it would taste good," Audrey replied. "Or is it that we are just starving."

"Well I wouldn't have thought to put walnuts and grapes in it either, but it's amazing what you can do with what you've got."

"My mother works in a Victory Garden back home, and she and some of the other women put together a recipe booklet using non-rationed foods. Some of them are really good."

"I'd classify this one as delicious," Nona said and relaxed against the back of the chair. "And thank you for letting me stay here tonight."

"You don't have to thank me. But that does remind me, let's get the news on." Audrey snapped on the radio by the bed and tuned in the Detroit station. She retrieved Cokes from the icebox and returned to the table. The announcer told them that any woman who tried the

Camay Mild-Soap Diet would see a big difference in her complexion before she used up that first cake of Camay.

Then, "We interrupt our regular broadcast to announce that Mayor Edward Jeffries Jr. and Governor Harry Kelly have asked for help from President Roosevelt in restoring order to the city of Detroit. The Mayor is urging everyone to stay home and off the streets for their safety. The police have reported a number of officers shot and gangs of Negroes looting and burning. I repeat: Stay in your homes and off the streets until further notice."

"There sure won't be any bus tomorrow," Audrey said.

"Reverend Jennings is going to be worried, but the phones are so restricted. I know we have to keep the lines open for the servicemen, but ten o'clock is so late to get to a phone."

Audrey checked her watch. "We could go to the community building after that, but it's always packed with people waiting and tonight might be even worse. Maybe I can get Lucy to let you use a company phone in accounting at lunch tomorrow."

"The Reverend is a good man of God, he'll add my safety to the prayers for peace in the city, but I would really appreciate being able to call him tomorrow. Thank you."

"Why do people have to fight and cause trouble when we should all be pulling together now? What kind of a world will we face if we lose this war?"

"My father's explanation," Nona replied, "would be that some people can't see past their own front porch."

Audrey smiled. "That's it, isn't it?"

"The news report made it sound like Negoes are causing all the problems. Do you think that's true?"

A test. So clear that even June the Oblivious wouldn't be able to miss it. "I think I understand why you asked me that," Audrey said. "But I wish you hadn't felt that you had to."

Nona's expression morphed from a frown into discomfort. "I had no right to say that, not after how good you've been to me. I'm sorry, Audrey." Audrey was shaking her head, but Nona continued. "I've never been actual friends with a white person. I don't know what to expect."

44

Or trust. Wasn't she right not to? How would she know without questioning, waiting, testing? After all, wasn't she being expected to trust a liar right now? "I've seen how you are treated differently. There were white people who didn't even show up to work when the bus didn't come. I doubt that their job was threatened. It's unfair. And I believe you when you say that it's been worse where you come from. If I were in your place, I would be so angry. How do you handle how you're treated without anger? Or do I just not see it?"

"We're all just *people*," Nona said, "more alike than many want to admit, all of us trying to make the best life we can for ourselves. Some handle fear and anger by striking out, but I don't see that it helps make things better."

For a long moment Audrey held Nona's gaze. Her thoughts, the doubt of her own ability to be honest with this woman kept her from saying anything. Nona's trust certainly deserved the truth, required the truth. Shouldn't she know who she was being asked to befriend? Nona wasn't like some casual lover who could, with merely physical desire, shimmy past lies and fears, subduing them with fire-hot heat, leaving them, without concern, to rise like a phoenix the next day. A friend, a real friend, didn't have that option. Lies must be exposed by truth, fears laid bare. Trust required it. That much Audrey knew.

Nona frowned. "What are you thinking about?"

"How much I needed a friend," she said, without lying. "And how we'd better get some sleep if we're going to keep up our pace tomorrow." True, every word. And avoiding what you didn't know much about was just smart. Audrey flipped off the radio. No Fibber McGee tonight.

"The sheets are almost fresh," she said. "I only slept on them one night. If you don't mind that, then the bed is yours."

"No," Nona replied. "I don't mind the sheets at all, but I won't take your bed. I'm used to sleeping on the floor."

Audrey tilted her head with mock seriousness. "This is my place—the only place where I can make the rules—and in my place no guest sleeps on the floor." She opened a drawer in a narrow bureau and handed Nona a clean nightgown. "There's a clean towel on the back

45

of the toilet," she said, motioning to the door at the end if the bed. "You can shower first while I get my bedding ready."

Nona rose without argument. "I hope I can be as good a friend as you deserve."

੭ ੭ ੭

Those words stayed with Audrey the whole next day. They begged to be addressed, especially after Reverend Jennings' report of armored cars and jeeps and troops with automatic weapons confronting rioters up and down Woodward meant another night away for Nona. Another night testing Audrey's honesty.

She wanted so much for those words to be worthy of a smile. She wanted to accept them, accept Nona, free and clear of lies and guilt. But there was only one way that she could do that. Thinking about it sucked the oxygen out of the air, but if there was to be a real friendship, it had to be done. That's what it would be if she was careful, if her purpose was pure and true and uncontaminated. A friendship. It would be all she needed from now on, a friend, this one. No need for another lover, or putting anyone else in danger ever again. She would learn to be a good friend, to be deserving.

Somewhere amid accepting the why and worrying about the how, she realized that entering into a love relationship hadn't been nearly as hard as this friendship. There were no sly lingering looks picked up and returned, or brushes of contact meant to send zings of recognition. No silent familiar nuances asking and answering. Truth understood, not spoken.

But this—she watched Nona clear the dishes from the table and put them in the sink—this was much harder than she had imagined.

"I'm doing up the dishes this time," Nona said, filling the sink with hot water. "Don't argue with me."

"I have learned that much about you."

"We've learned that about each other," Nona replied.

Audrey nodded to herself. Indeed they had. And more. "I've learned a lot *from* you," she added, as she dried a dish and placed it on the shelf next to the sink.

Nona handed Audrey the last of the dishes with a look of mild surprise. "What could you have learned from me?"

"If you really want to know, then dry your hands and get comfortable."

Nona's smile was like that of a young girl waiting for secrets to be told. "Did you have sleepovers when you were a little girl?" she asked, and settled at the head of the bed to hug her knees. "This feels like a sleepover."

Audrey claimed the spot at the foot of the bed. She sat cross-legged and leaned folded arms comfortably on her knees. "The bastion for the honesty of youth. Here we are," she added and smiled.

"I had a Catholic friend," Nona said, "who thought of sleepovers as precursors to the confessional without the Hail Marys."

"I'm grateful I'm not Catholic, then." Hail Marys couldn't have atoned for all her lies, or the guilt, or for her own toxicity. Surely not. Nothing could. "And I'm grateful to know you. It's made me look at myself in a way I haven't before."

"I hope you see good things, because that's what I see."

"Good or bad, the things I see now are true. Things I have to own now."

Nona cocked her head and waited.

"I watch you deal with things that would make most people give up on their dreams, and end up settling for what others want for them. You have plenty of reasons to give up and no options if you don't."

"Options?"

"You can't hide what makes reaching your goals so hard. You can't change the color of your skin to make life easier."

"No," Nona replied, "but that's obvious enough for even Miss Oblivious, wouldn't you say?"

"But she doesn't know *my* options. No one does. I hide behind my options because I'm not as strong as you are."

"I don't believe that. You're here working on your own, and making your own decisions. You don't have to put up with people criticizing what you wear and where you work. You could have stayed home and gotten married. You can go back home any time, or get married and

47

quit working and take care of a family. You have easier paths that you could take."

"Ones that are supposed to make me happy," Audrey said.

"Only we can decide that, nobody knows but us."

"But I don't know, not like you do. I don't have a plan like you. You know what you want, and what will make you happy. I envy that about you."

"I'm sure nobody's ever envied me," Nona replied. "They've been proud of me, my family's proud of me."

"I wish I could say that, too. I'm glad you can." Audrey drew her knees to her chest and wrapped her arms around them to match Nona. "How are we supposed to know what will make us happy? How do *you* know?"

Nona hesitated for a moment. "I think if you want something enough, even finding a way to get there makes you happy. Being here, this leg of my journey makes me happy because I know it's getting me closer to the life I want."

"I'm here now because I needed something bigger than my own worries. Here, every day, every rivet, every piece we finish is more important than me. I never worry about why or whether it's the right thing to do. It isn't about me, it's much more important. So, I haven't had to think about me at all."

Nona rested her chin on her knees and offered only her undivided attention.

Audrey continued. "Until I met you, and you made me look at myself again."

"So is that good?"

Audrey shrugged. "It's . . . uncomfortable. Makes me realize how strange it is to rather be thinking about production numbers and war than to think about what I want in my life."

"Not so strange," Nona said. "You got a guy over there in this war, of course you're thinking more about that than yourself."

Truth. Just a little, just enough. She deserved that, any good friend deserved that. "I," Audrey began, but the usual warning caused her to hesitate. She began again. "I don't have a guy over there." She watched Nona's expression change—an opening, a widening—more inquisitive than questioning, if Audrey read it correctly. "A lot of people, like Mac and June and Janice, don't understand why a woman would choose to work in a bomber plant when she could more easily support the war at home. But, if you've got a guy serving, or kids to support, it's a lot easier for them to justify it. It's only for now, only until the war is over, and then everything will return to normal. It's darn close to acceptable," she said and smiled.

"So you lied to them."

Audrey nodded. "I *lie* to a lot of people."

"But not me?"

"No, I won't lie to you." A promise, said out loud now, that she had every intention of keeping. But tonight's offering of truth was all she was willing to chance right now. "Your friendship means a lot to me," she said, swinging her legs off the bed. "And I don't want you to hate me tomorrow if we don't get some good sleep tonight." She pulled the extra bedding off the end of the bed. "Jack said that Mac is pushing some pretty crazy numbers for us to meet—and not just for tomorrow. Numbers we're going to need to meet every day. They need more planes and like Jack says—"

"By God, we're gonna give 'em to 'em."

It brought a wide smile to Audrey's face.

🙞 🙞 🙞

Heavy clouds muted the moonlight finding its way through the slit between the drape panels covering the window. The room was darker than usual, and quieter than usual. The neighbors on the other side of the wall had gone to bed early. The only sounds were the ticking of the alarm clock on the floor next to her pillow and Nona's soft rhythmic breathing from the bed next to her.

Audrey opened her eyes again, trying to keep the vision from haunting still another night. Sometimes it worked, when she took inventory of her blessings—her own space, her health, her work, her friend, her choices—forcing them to soothe the pain of the memories. Other times she would listen to the radio, and let the company of now-familiar voices distract her. She would fill her thoughts trying to imagine what they looked like while they talked her to sleep. But times like tonight, despite being exhausted, nothing stopped the memory, or the vision.

Blue eyes twinkling with laughter stirred wondrous sensations that she couldn't stop, started a love they couldn't stop. An all-consuming love, exciting and toxic. It took them by surprise, sunk its barbs so deeply that neither of them could pull away. They both knew that there would be no other love for them. They wanted nothing more, nothing less. It was this love or nothing. And they claimed it, claimed each other for as long as they could, never believing it would end.

The vision, so close to her that it was almost tactile, tricked her into believing it hadn't ended. And with the vision came the memories, the only thing that tamed the pain—beginning with those sweetest of all, the beginning of love.

It was her eyes, it had started with her eyes. She used them better than words. They pulled Audrey in, soft blue, sending shocks through her chest. She couldn't look away as they reached in, asking for permission, answering with a kiss. Audrey closed her eyes. She was there with her in the dim light of Velma's bedroom, answering the questions for the first time. It would be a woman, yes, only a woman. This woman. Velma.

She had loved the way Velma laughed, light bursts of joy, and the way she whispered her name. She had loved the quickness of her mind and the way her skin felt under her touch. Tonight she would remember the way love felt, and the comfort of falling asleep in Velma's arms. It would bring her peace until she slept.

Chapter 8

It was totally unexpected, the way being with so many other girls living the same shame, facing the same decisions, had changed her focus and centered Ruth's world in a different way. The grand Crittenton plan was for her to focus on her own shortcomings so that they could fulfill their mission of reshaping the wayward and educating the ignorant. What she found, though, tucked discreetly between the tight daily regimen and beyond the demeaning atmosphere, was that focusing on something and someone other than herself was what made her stronger.

Susan had been the start of it with her easy manner, talking and listening and winning the confidence of those around her. Ruth, too, was a good listener and it didn't take long before she knew the stories. The *whys* repeated themselves over and over—he was going off to war and might never come back; we were, we are in love; it was only one time. Predictable, too, were the questions and the fears. Would people know when they went back home? How painful would childbirth be? Would she ever be able to forgive herself for giving her baby away? Girls from different states with more in common than they were different, except for one girl.

"It's Amelia," Susan said, walking quickly past Ruth on her way toward the back entrance. "There's something wrong."

Ruth followed on her heels. "What happened?"

Susan shook her head, then spoke over her shoulder. "She left the laundry room crying."

Ruth caught up with Susan at the back door. "Did someone say something?"

"I don't know. I was on my way to meet her and saw her running out of the room. At fourteen she's not going to handle things as well as us old ladies."

"I never felt so old," Ruth replied. "It gives me perspective, though."

"There she is," Susan said, pointing toward the far edge of the yard.

They walked quickly across freshly cut grass until they caught up with Amelia. Neither of them had to say a word. As soon as she realized they were beside her, Amelia turned into Susan's arms.

"It's okay," Susan said softly. "Everything's going to be okay."

"What has you so upset?" asked Ruth as she stroked the long, honey-colored hair. "What happened?"

Amelia stepped back and wiped her eyes with the palm of her hand. "I just want to disappear. I don't want to be here. I don't want to be anywhere."

"Well, you are not the first girl to feel like that," Ruth offered. "I've had those moments, too, and they are only that, moments."

Susan smoothed the hair from Amelia's forehead. "Come on," she said, "let's walk back and sit outside to talk so that they don't think we're trying to escape."

The corners of Ruth's mouth curled into a half-smile. "I wonder if anyone *has* ever escaped from this place."

The three of them walked slowly, silently back to the blue metal chairs at the back of the building. They seated themselves closely together and spoke in quiet voices.

Ruth began. "The most important thing we can do while we're here is to watch out for each other. Agreed?" Both Susan and Amelia nodded. "I'll make a pledge right now," she said, putting her hand palm down in the circle of space between them. "I will listen with an open heart, and keep to myself anything I'm told, and help you both in any way I can."

Susan placed her hand on Ruth's and added, "I pledge the same."

Her hand hesitated for only a second, then Amelia moved it quickly over the others. "Me, too," she said. "I pledge, too."

It had taken weeks, a long time in Crittenton count. Weeks of watching a shy, frightened young girl try to find her way alone in a place that reminded her daily of what an embarrassment she was and how she was responsible for the condition she was in. And as difficult as it was for Ruth to manage her own adjustment, it was infinitely more difficult to watch someone like Amelia. So, during that time, the two old ladies of the Home had watched out for the youngest. Now, finally, maybe she would trust them with the demons that frightened her.

"When I first got here," Susan began, "there was only Mrs. Stranton to welcome me and show me around. If I hadn't already been frightened and unsure, I sure would have been, only minutes after walking in the front door. As soon as I settled some, I promised myself that the next girl through that door would see a friendlier face. Mrs. Stranton didn't seem to mind, and I found out quickly that making other girls feel better, in turn, made me feel better. I'm going to hope that someone takes over for me after I leave." She met Amelia's eyes briefly before they dropped away.

"I can't imagine my first day here without you," Ruth directed at Susan. "And every day since, you've made it tolerable. More than that, you've made me feel like maybe the whole world hasn't turned its back on me."

"You make me feel like that, too," Amelia said. "Both of you do."

"Then you know you can trust us," Susan replied.

"Things aren't as sad or impossible," Ruth added, "or scary when you share them."

"And I feel horrible," Susan said reaching for Amelia's hand, "seeing you cry, and wondering if there was something I could have done, maybe to stop it or keep it from happening again."

Amelia shook her head. "There was nothing you could do. It was Mrs. Stranton."

"She works here only to torture us," Susan said.

Amelia nodded. "She said no one will ever have sympathy for women full of selfishness who try to ruin the lives of young men."

"Sure," Ruth said, her words oozing with sarcasm, "we put ourselves in this condition just to ruin some guy's life."

Amelia's eyes moistened and seemed to beg for belief. "But I didn't."

"Of course you didn't," Susan said. "I dare say that none of us here did."

"I was only being sarcastic, Amelia. They can call us what they want, Able Grables, sharecroppers, it doesn't matter. It doesn't make it so."

"We're here for a reason," Susan added, "so that the people back home don't know. Sometimes it seems like a long time, but if we put up with how they treat us here, we can go home and start fresh."

Amelia lowered her head. "Maybe you can."

Words Ruth had hoped not to hear. They all but verified the fear she and Susan had for Amelia. "Are you afraid that the boy is still going to be around? Are you worried that you won't be able to avoid him?"

"No." It was a fierceness of tone that they had not heard from her. Still, tears welled in Amelia's eyes. "You don't understand. No one does."

"Then tell us," Susan said. "We want to understand."

Amelia wiped the wetness from flushed cheeks with both hands.

"It's alright, Amelia," Ruth said. "You can tell us, whatever it is."

"You won't believe me," she said, peering at them through watery blue eyes. "No one will."

"Why on earth wouldn't we believe you?" Ruth asked.

"If my mother doesn't believe me, why would anyone else?"

"We're going through this with you," Susan replied. "I think that allows us to believe things that others don't understand."

"You can trust us," Ruth added. "We need to trust each other."

What had begun as a whisper, connecting Amelia's age, her slight build, her shyness, was now a belief Ruth could no longer keep quiet. If Amelia couldn't say it, Ruth would ask it. "There's a big difference between a boy talking you into doing something, and physically *forcing* you to do something you didn't want to do." Ruth waited but Amelia refused to meet her eyes. "Is that what happened, Amelia?"

Tears now streamed down Amelia's cheeks. Her eyes remained down, her nod unnecessary.

"Geez," Susan whispered.

"No, just say it, Susan," Ruth replied. "*Jesus.* Because whoever it is, he needs to answer to the Big Man."

Susan added, "He should be answering to *someone.* Is he a lot older than you?"

Another nod. Eyes refusing contact. Tears turning to soft sobs.

All of it fuel that sparked Ruth's need for answers. "And you told your mother, told her who it was? Did she confront him? Did he deny it?"

Tinges of pink now framed the blue of Amelia's eyes as they met Ruth's and then Susan's.

"It's okay," Susan said. "You don't need to say any more if you don't want."

Ruth watched what she assumed was relief as Amelia closed her eyes and took deeper, longer breaths to regain control. Susan was probably right, they had pushed hard enough, expected maybe more than a frightened young girl could manage. The anger that had gained its validity needed to stay right where it was, with Ruth.

But her assumption was wrong. And so was Susan's.

"Nothing will change," Amelia said. "He's still going to be there, and they still won't believe me."

"Who is he?" Ruth asked.

"My uncle," she replied. "He lives right next door."

"Sweet Jesus." Ruth shot an angry look at Susan. "No wonder."

Susan leaned close and wrapped her arms around Amelia, who was crying softly. "Thank you," she said softly. "We're right here. You can trust us with anything." Susan met Ruth's eyes and read her lips, *What are we going to do?* Her answer, mouthed silently, *I don't know.*

Chapter 9

No doubt every girl in the Home held some anger, mostly at herself. Each time they looked in a mirror, did they see the weakness, the indecision, the doubts and fears that put them there? Did they see what Ruth saw? Maybe they did. But could any of them imagine what Amelia must see? And the anger that Ruth felt now had to be harnessed, fashioned somehow into useful, constructive energy, for Amelia's sake.

For the next few weeks both Susan and Ruth worked to do just that. Their own worries were set aside as they found a new focus—protection took precedence. They had become a force, one that Amelia depended on and one that even Mrs. Stranton couldn't affect. Every day they claimed their back-row seats in class and sandwiched their young charge between them. With their heads down and pencils deceptively busy they kept Amelia's attention on mocking notes and drawings and off unwarranted reprimands and demeaning advice. Chat time was religiously kept every evening and questions were answered as if from experience—confident and reassuring. Confidence garnered for Amelia. It was about her, for her.

And it was working. The time had allowed her trust in them to set up solid, for smiles to finally ease into her days. Young fears, different from Ruth's or Susan's, now had a place to rest, a place where even probables were hushed. She was comfortable and safe.

But like everything else about being at the Home, it was measured in months, months of separation, months of pregnancy, months of friendship. Measured, anguished over, trusted in, and then gone. That morning, what had only been real in delayed thought, had become gut-wrenchingly real. Susan had delivered, and today she was going home.

Susan sat on the edge of her bed, everything she had come with packed once again in the suitcase next to her. She had readied herself in the ways she could, with traveling dress and open-toed shoes, hair brushed and shiny and pulled up neatly on the sides. But her eyes said the unsayable

Ruth saw it, the trepidation, the sadness. And the same worry that this day was waving like a white flag. There wasn't much more Susan would be able to do now. Her support, her strength, her advice would be greatly diminished within minutes. She knew that.

It was up to Ruth to face it, to own the weight of it, to give in to the reality of it. It was her turn to face the fears, the decisions, the unknown. And she would, just as Susan had. But could Amelia?

"Was it a boy or a girl?" Amelia asked, leaning close to Susan on the bed.

"A boy," she replied. "They wouldn't tell me, but Nurse Lillian whispered to me before I left the hospital." She took Amelia's hand. "They're afraid knowing will make us change our minds, and try to find them later."

"We'll never know, will we?" Amelia asked. "What their lives are going to be like, what—"

"It's probably better that we don't know," Ruth said.

Susan brought her eyes back to Ruth's. "I thought so, too, before he was born."

Ruth's focus changed quickly. She didn't believe for a moment what she had just said. She had said it for Amelia's sake, to in some way lessen the worry and hopefully ease past today with as little anxiety as possible. But maybe Susan was right, to let Amelia start dealing with the inevitable now. It wasn't anything that any of them could avoid. "Of course we're going to wonder," she said. "It's a natural thing to wonder." She slid the wooden straight-back chair closer to the bed and sat for what she knew was their last chance to really talk. "Every night I lie awake trying to decide what I should do, what will be best in the long term. Susan, you and I have talked about it a lot and I've talked with Nurse Lillian, too. Do I fight to keep my baby, even though I don't know where I'll live or how I would provide for a child? Is it fair to keep my baby from having a good home and parents who can provide everything that I can't? You were right, it's not fair, it's selfish."

"Sometimes," Susan added, "love just isn't enough. It's better that *we* make the sacrifice than to expect our babies to."

"We can't feel bad about our decision," Ruth said, taking Amelia's other hand. "We'll all wonder about them, I'm sure, forever. But we have to remind ourselves that we did what was best for our babies."

Tears welled in Amelia's eyes. Susan put her arms around Amelia's shoulders and pulled her close. "You're going to be fine," she said. "Everything is going to be all right." She held her there for a few minutes and made eye contact with Ruth. Then she wiped the tears from Amelia's cheeks. "Will you do something for me?" Amelia lifted her head. "Will you go down and see if they've pulled the car around yet?"

Amelia nodded and rose from the bed.

As soon as she had left the room, Ruth asked, "Do you believe that, knowing what she has to return home to?"

It was more than tiredness or Susan's own personal anguish that Ruth saw in her eyes. And there was no need for Susan to put it into words.

"What are we going to do?" Ruth continued.

"We have just over five months to figure something out, and I'm going to be three states away trying to put my life back together. And soon you're going to be . . . where *are* you going to be?"

"I'm not going back home." For the first time the words sounded sure, confident. Ruth said them without hesitation. "Nurse Lillian's mother-in-law lives in Ypsilanti, not far from here, and she has a friend who will let me rent her extra bedroom. There are lots of jobs for women right now, I'll find something."

Susan retrieved a small pad of paper and a pencil from her purse. "Here," she said, "this is my address. Write me as soon as you are out of here."

Ruth took the slip of paper and nodded. "I'll get Amelia's address and make sure she has ours before I leave. She's going to be so scared."

"You said you would talk to Nurse Lillian. Are you going to tell her Amelia's secret?"

"I want Amelia to tell her. She has to have someone to trust after I leave."

"If she doesn't tell her," Susan said, "you have to, Ruth."

"I know," she replied. "I won't leave her to do this alone."

Susan rose from the edge of the bed, no sign of the bright smile that had first greeted Ruth, and hugged her tightly. "I hate to leave you alone, too," she said softly.

Ruth squeezed her arms around her friend and hugged her silently for a long moment. Alone was something she had felt for a very long time. Susan had been a temporary reprieve, but Ruth knew to expect no more than that. She knew that temporary might always be the best she could expect, even for friendship.

"I'm going to miss you," Ruth said, relinquishing their hug to meet Susan's eyes. They were liquid with tears, like her own.

"We'll stay in touch," Susan said and wiped her tears with the back of her hand. "Don't forget to write as soon as you can."

"I won't. And thank you for being such a good friend when I needed one most."

"Hey, we Able Gables have to watch out for each other." Susan finally offered a smile. "If only you could keep me company on the ride to the train." She picked up her suitcase and turned toward the door. "I'm off to endure my last twenty minutes of demeaning insults from Mrs. Stranton." She took a deep breath and straightened her shoulders. "Here I go."

Ruth returned the smile. "I envy you."

Chapter 10

What the men carry, what the men eat, the ships they sail in,
that all comes from the unanimity of our war effort, down to
the average citizen. And I believe that it is due to the magnifi-
cent effort in all our countries, but one which must be kept up
very clearly and definitely to the high pitch that it has now
arrived at. We cannot afford in any way to assume that military
and naval, or air men can win this war alone. They need the
backing of the people back home . . .

Franklin D. Roosevelt, August 1943

Despite heavy U.S. aircraft losses over Kiel, Allied forces continued
to bomb Sicily and the Italian mainland in anticipation of an invasion,
and America continued its "island hopping" strategy in the Southwest
Pacific.

More bombers were needed, and the plant providing them faster
than any in the country was Willow Run. Sorensen's ingenious adap-
tation of Ford's assembly line had silenced the critics. It wasn't just
Star Man Mac demanding the increased production from the crews,
it was the expectations of FDR himself. To a person, there wasn't one
willing to disappoint the President. And most of them, like Audrey,
took the challenge personally.

No one could miss it. The banner, stretching half the length of a
wing, was hung above a midwing station and proudly displayed the
crew's top daily number. The intent was clear, their goal each day was
to beat that number. The gauntlet had been thrown down.

The challenge was accepted. Mac's insistent shouts over the whine
of the machines were even less relevant than usual. Even June's less
than competitive nature couldn't avoid the bump of adrenaline as she

passed by the banner. Her question as she emerged from the tool room was all any of them needed to hear. "What was *our* best number?" Their mission was set. The day saw the beginning of a drive that suffered the heat and exhaustion, the aches and pain, and ignored distraction for one common goal. The race was on with no finish line in sight.

"Break!" Mac bellowed over Jack's shoulder. "Now."

Jack straightened, checked his watch, and repeated the call to the rest of the crew. "Break time."

Mac cocked his head and took a step toward Jack. "Salt and water, dammit. Ain't nobody droppin' dead on *my* shift."

Jack turned away abruptly and motioned the crew away from the station.

They collected the required salt and water and gathered at the break table. Audrey took a gulp of water and tried to swallow the salt tablet on the first try. She shuddered as the rough tablet stuck to the back of her throat, then squeezed her eyes shut and took another gulp.

"Ach, I hate these things," she said, and downed the rest of the water without a breath.

"I know," Jack said, "but believe me, you don't want your guts tied into a knot so tight you're huggin' your knees to try to stop the pain."

She wasn't questioning the reasons or doubting the consequences. August in Michigan only amplified the heat and humidity within the plant, and sweat-soaked, heavy blue coveralls and sweat dripping from nose and chin testified to the need. But it didn't make swallowing salt tablets twice a day any more enjoyable.

"Any reason we have to take the full ten-minute break?" Audrey asked.

Jack followed her gaze in the direction of the banner. "Can't think of a one," he replied. "Anyone else need a full break?"

No one hesitated. The crew moved immediately to return to their station.

⁓ ⁓ ⁓

At the end of the day the all-important number, the sweat-proved evidence of their collective effort, hung in the air on Jack's shout. "Seven."

Audrey, relieved and exhausted, tipped her head back and shouted, "We did it!"

And Bennie's rare response, "D-d-damn."

"Seven full pieces," added June. "A half-piece better than our best."

They returned their tools and aprons to the tool room, and Audrey wiped the sweat from her face and neck with her headscarf. "I feel like we should celebrate," she said, "do something to reward ourselves. But I don't even have the energy to take a shower."

"We'd all better try to get some food down and get a good night's sleep," Jack said. "We put out seven today and Mac's gonna expect no less than that tomorrow."

"We *can* do it again," Nona added. "We're the best crew on the line."

Their moments of exhilaration settled quickly into the tired space that followed a normal work day. June left to go home to her boys and dinner, waiting. Bennie would stop at his sister's and deliver bomber pictures to his nephew and eat birthday cake. And Jack needed to pick up Lucy and make it to dinner with his in-laws.

Jack started for the exit, steps quicker than his usual stride, then stopped and came back a few. "Oh," he said, "I can drop you off at your place first, Audrey."

"Do you still want to see my new place?" Nona asked. "Or are you too tired?"

"I'm exhausted and hungry and absolutely want to see your place," Audrey replied. "You go ahead, Jack, family's waiting." She watched as he nodded and started off again, and then called after him, "I wish there was some way that Lucy could hurry things along. The suspense is gonna kill me."

"A Christmas baby, that's what she's thinkin'."

Nona offered a bright smile. "Come on," she said, "the bus will take us to Michigan Avenue and we can walk from there."

∽ ∽ ∽

It wasn't a pleasant experience, the ride to town. Not because a very large man with body odor that could permeate steel pressed her against the rail frame of the bus. Or the man behind her with the rattling cough that moved the hair at the back of her head. It was because what was left of her fragile naivety dissolved with Nona in the back of the bus.

She had kept moving down the aisle after Audrey claimed a seat near the front, passing more empty seats on her way to the rear. She hadn't said anything, hadn't warned Audrey that reality could be so unpleasant. The moment that the difference for them had become painfully real was when Audrey turned to see the last of the passengers walk to the rear where Nona and two other Negroes stood to give up their seats. There was no asking, no infirming need—only expectation and compliance. Audrey watched her friend balance herself in the middle of the aisle, eyes straight ahead, only a tentative hand on the edge of the seatback as the bus rolled toward town.

Audrey couldn't stand to look any longer, couldn't absorb what she saw, couldn't *accept* the acceptance. Worse, she could not stomach that she was part of it. She rode the rest of the way with her forehead against the window.

Michigan Avenue was lined with industry and businesses, and was home to the plant personnel's favorite restaurant, The Bomber. Enticing smells escaping from the vents of the building as they walked past brought back the hunger pains that the bus ride had stifled.

"I know you're hungry," Nona began, "and I think I can finally handle some food. Those salt tablets really destroy the appetite, don't they?"

Audrey stopped and took Nona's arm. "Come on, then, we'll eat at The Bomber." It might have been the hesitation, or the expression on Nona's face that Audrey had no name for, but she knew before Nona told her.

"Audrey, I can't go in there," she replied. "Look, there's a grocery by my neighborhood. I don't know what Mrs. Bailey has on hand, so we'll stop and get something to fix."

Of course it was the thing to do, the only thing to do. Another lift in the fog, a painful reveal. Audrey nodded.

They stopped at the grocery where Audrey ignored the stares of Negoes wondering why she was in their store, and continued on to a wood-clad two-story house in the middle of a residential block.

"I'm so lucky," Nona said, leading Audrey to the side of the house.

She used a key and let them in. "Mrs. Bailey's daughter was married last month and renting out her room helps her pay the bills. Mr. Bailey passed two years ago, keeled over of a heart attack shoveling snow from the walk."

The kitchen was small, white metal canisters of staples taking up much of the counter space. Nona placed the groceries next to the sink and motioned for Audrey to sit at the tiny table, barely large enough for two plates.

"Mrs. Bailey's at a prayer meeting tonight." Nona began washing and slicing and putting together a garden salad. "I'm actually getting an appetite back," she said, retrieving a frying pan from under the counter and preparing it for sliced potatoes and ham.

The distraction allowed Audrey time to weigh her discomfort, and to question her suspicion of Nona's timing. Was it merely a coincidence that Nona's landlady was away this evening? Was she right to personalize it, to think that she had jumped into Nona's shoes? And if she was right, maybe she needed to redefine the bounds of friendship, but she wondered if she had the right to ask.

Amid small talk and relishing the taste of dinner, Audrey let the questions form. No rush to ask them, or to answer them. No rush to trade away the easiness and Nona's excitement in showing off her room.

The floorboards groaned as they entered the little upstairs bedroom. Nona smiled and flopped onto the iron-rail bed. "Welcome to my palace," she said.

Audrey looked around the room with its wooden blanket chest at the foot of the bed and tall bureau sitting between two narrow windows and replied, "Perfect. It is, Nona. It's perfect."

"And clean and dry," she said and laid back on the bed. "And so comfy. No more sleeping on the basement floor."

"And your own space," Audrey said and smiled. "I know how good *that* feels."

"Yes." Nona sat up and motioned for Audrey to sit on the bed. "A place where I can be alone with myself. I can listen to whatever radio programs I want, or read at night, or," she raised her eyebrows and grinned, "or traipse around here all evening without undergarments."

Audrey's eyes twinkled with amusement. "I talk back to the radio. I say things that would turn proper heads. It feels really good."

"Then I'll do it, too," Nona replied. "Oh, there are so many things I've wanted to say. I want to talk back to ol' Alan Kent and ask him how his Camay Soap Diet's going to help me get a degree. I want to talk back to Mayor Jeffries." Nona sighed and relaxed her shoulders. "I just want to talk back."

"*Yes.* And where else? Have you ever even talked back to your parents?"

"Only once," Nona said. "But doing my siblings' chores on top of my own made me think twice the next time I felt the urge."

"I ate soap."

Nona burst into laughter, and Audrey joined her. "How many times?" Nona finally managed.

"Once for back talk, once for a word unbecoming." She watched Nona stifle another laugh. "I suppose I should have been grateful. My cousins got the switch—more than a few times."

"Well, you can tell me anything you want," Nona said, "unbecoming or not, and I promise there will be no soap in sight."

Audrey allowed her smile to soften. Her eyes stayed with Nona's. "But it's not the same for you, is it?"

Nona hesitated a moment before saying, "I don't understand."

"I think there are things you won't say to me because I'm white." When Nona didn't respond, Audrey continued. "Because I won't understand, or because you don't trust me?"

Nona shook her head. "No. I trust you, but there are things that I can't expect you to understand."

"Like waiting for today when your landlady is away to show me your room. I saw the stares at the grocery, and realized that you hurried us out of there. You won't have to find a polite way to explain that you can do little to change the discomfort that I feel being in your neighborhood, visiting your world. I understand that much, and that it is only a small part of what you deal with. But there are things that I endure that you may not be able to fully understand, too. Do we have a friendship that can survive those differences?"

"I'm willing to find out if you are."

Audrey nodded. "It has been a long time since I have had a friend that I can talk to."

"Then you talk and I'll listen."

It was the right decision. It had to be. She'd picked the perfect person. It needed to be a woman like Nona, someone sure of her own needs, confident. Knowing exactly what she wanted for her life and going after it. And there was no hiding her struggle, the challenges to her goals were right out there for everyone to recognize. It was time to trust at least this one woman with a struggle of her own that had been hidden for so long.

"Do you remember when I told you that I hide behind my options?" Nona nodded, and Audrey continued. "What I struggle with isn't obvious. I can keep it private and no one needs to know. And I lie to do that. I lie because I don't have the courage to face things that you face—or maybe worse."

The smooth skin of Nona's brow pinched into dark lines of concern, but she said nothing.

Audrey hesitated. She had never said it out loud, and for a moment it felt as though someone else was about to give up her secret. It didn't sound like her voice, it was surprisingly more determined, more sure. "Have you ever been in love?" her new voice asked.

Nona's concern seemed to ease some. "No," she replied, "not yet. There was one boy at school, though, as handsome as a girl could want. He ran track. I loved a lot about him, how hard he worked and his polite manners." She offered a little smile and added, "I loved kissing him and how he made me feel. But, eventually I realized how easy it was to leave my books behind and give him all of my attention. It started to feel like I was giving up me to be with him. I wasn't ready to do that. I'm still not."

"I never thought about it that way," Audrey replied. "I don't know that I could have. I just fell in love and nothing mattered except being together and keeping the secret." It was out there now, the need for explanation. There was no avoiding it now, only a moment to gather the words, and wait for the inevitable question.

It took Nona longer than expected, maybe out of respect or just courtesy for something clearly difficult to talk about. Audrey overcame the urge to pull her eyes away, to avoid as she had done all of her life.

Nona spoke with a softness in her voice and in her eyes. "Are you afraid that when I know the secret that it will make me dislike you?"

"I am afraid of that, and it might. But it isn't fair to expect an honest friendship from you and not offer you the same."

"So, just tell me," Nona said, "and don't worry because, unless you're a murderer, I won't run."

"A murderer, huh?" Audrey replied without an accompanying smile. "That could be a matter of interpretation." She waited a few seconds for a reaction, but Nona remained unmoved. "Because of me, of my love, someone's life will never be the same. All I knew was that I loved her, more than I ever imagined I could love." The tears came without warning, welling quickly and spilling down Audrey's cheeks. "That love . . . my love, destroyed her."

Nona leaned forward and reached for Audrey's hand. She grasped it tightly. "No," she said, "I can't believe love can destroy anything or anyone. Hate destroys, Audrey, not love."

Audrey dropped her head. Her tears continued, dropping onto the back of Nona's hand. "That's what love did," she replied quietly. "That's what caused the hate." Audrey lifted her eyes to Nona's. "We couldn't stop how we felt. It was wrong, but we couldn't change it. We tried not seeing each other, but we couldn't."

"Do you believe it was wrong to love her?"

The question was unexpected. It challenged her answer, unsettled the settled in her mind. Of course it was wrong. Everything she had read said that it was. It wasn't the normal, natural plan. "Everything in my head says that it is."

"But?"

Audrey slipped her hand free and leaned back against the foot of the bed. She wiped the wetness from her cheeks. "But it doesn't change what I feel here," she said, placing her hand over her heart.

"Do you want my opinion?" Nona asked.

"Of course I do. I never thought I would be able to talk to anyone about it."

"You're my friend, Audrey. We can talk to each other when we can't talk to anyone else. So, I'm going to tell you what I think. If we listened to most people, even our families or people from our church, we wouldn't *be* friends. Mac and a lot of people like him think that women should not be in the work force, should not wear trousers, or have their own bank accounts. Are we wrong because we do? And what should I do if I find the man who loves me and respects my goals and I want to share my life with him—and he's white? What am I to do then?"

It was an easy answer, knowing what she knew of Nona. "Love him. Find a way to spend your life together. I can't imagine you doing anything *other* than that."

Nona tilted her head. "Despite everything that would be said and every danger we would face? Marrying a white man is illegal, and considered just as wrong as your relationship was."

"So maybe like me you would love once in your lifetime—love as well as you can and for as long as you can."

Chapter 11

The war is now reaching the stage where we shall all have to
look to large casualty lists—dead, wounded, and missing. War
entails just that. There is no easy road to victory. And the end
is not yet in sight.

Franklin D. Roosevelt, Fireside Chat, December 24, 1943

The fall months had come and gone, leaves shriveled and dropped,
and night temperatures bottomed to freezing—almost a blessing from
the heat and humidity of summer. Yet, the true blessing in those
months, possible through her friendship with Nona, was the blessing
of honesty. It was limited, and less visceral than building Liberators
to win a war, but honesty was what validated some measure of
Audrey's own goodness. She valued it, never thought she'd have it
again in her life, and carefully protected it.

The blessing, and cold nights snuggled beneath the feather
comforter, allowed sounder sleep than she had had in what seemed
like years. And it was needed.

American B-24s were needed on numerous fronts—Germany,
Sicily, Rangoon, Tarawa, Rabaul, and the Mid-Atlantic. The numbers
were huge—50 bombers for the air raid on Wilhelmshaven naval base,
160 in strikes on German power and water facilities in Vemork,
Norway.

The demand was enormous, the pressure to increase production
greater than ever. Hours and shifts were added, efficiency streamlined.
Every station, every crew, every part of the assembly increased
efficiency, and the numbers continued to go up.

Audrey pulled on her wool jacket and picked up her keys to wait
by the door for Jack. She stared through the small front window at

the morning, still hours from dawn. She slipped her hands in her pockets, where the unopened letter from her mother had remained since yesterday. It had been too late and she was too tired to read it the night before. Today on a break, she promised herself. It had come three days before Christmas, and it would hold no surprises. Her mother would say "short of those fighting this war abroad, families should gather together for the holiday." The same thing that she had said about Thanksgiving. All those in her family within reasonable travel distance, and Audrey was, would be spending the holiday at her grandparents' big house in Adrian. "If only," it would read, followed by half a page dedicated to what a young woman could do right at home to help the war effort, "if only" her daughter would consider the importance of family. What would not be mentioned was the discomfort her mother felt in having to explain, yet again, why Audrey chose to leave home alone, unmarried. Chose to make life difficult for herself, and worse, to spend holidays with someone else's family. The message was unwritten but it could not have been more clear.

Minutes later, the lights of Jack's car glistened across fresh falling snow covering a crusted layer of ice from the night before. Audrey stepped carefully down the walk and around the front of the car to the passenger seat. She hadn't even closed the door before an unshaven and disheveled Jack announced, "It's a girl!"

"Oh, Jack. Oh, wow! When did she have it? Is Lucy okay? What's her name? You must be so excited."

"Well, yeah," he replied, and added a wide grin. "Yeah, excited, tired, *proud*. But poor Lucy, fourteen hours of labor while I'm just pacin' the waiting room. She's good, though, just exhausted. Her mother's at the hospital with her, she said she'll probably sleep most of the day." It was already more than Audrey had heard him say in one sitting, and he chattered on. "Evelyn Rose, that's my little girl. She's a beauty, Audrey. She *is* a beauty."

≈ ≈ ≈

Pure excitement and an overload of adrenaline was the only explanation for how Jack kept the unrelenting pace at work. Audrey caught him a number of times during the morning with eyes glued to the job, sweat glistening on his facial stubble and the biggest smile on his face. It made Audrey smile, too.

Lunch break found Jack with a cart sandwich in one hand and cigars in the other, making the rounds of the lunch tables and spreading the good news.

"That is a happy man," June said to nods at their lunch table.

"He must have said Evie Rose three dozen times already," Audrey added. "And that doesn't count how many times he said her name in the car on the way to work."

"Lucy should be even happier," June said, lifting her head with an odd tilt. "She gets to stay home now and take care of her baby and her husband. I can't wait until this war is over and I can go back home and take care of *my* husband and kids. That's where a woman ought to be. There's nothing more important in this world, if you ask me."

Not to be outdone, Janice added, "As soon as my Bobby gets home we're not wastin' any time startin' *our* family. He wants lots of kids, and that's just fine with me."

June made a point to look right past Nona and said, "How about you, Audrey, how many kids does Bradley want?"

She felt the curtain pull around her secret, shroud it and protect it. "We haven't talked about it," she replied.

"I don't know that you have to have a number in mind," Janice added. "Just let 'em come when they will, I say. Let God decide."

"That's a little premature," Audrey said. "I'm not sure I'm going to marry him."

"You going to fool around," June warned, "and end up an old maid? Once you start losin' your looks, the pickin' gets slim. If you got yourself a good one now, you need to get that ring on your finger."

Bennie was eating his lunch and quiet as usual. And the girl talk might have ended there if Janice hadn't decided to include Nona. She looked past June and across the table where Nona was finishing the last few bites of lunch. "What about you, Nona," she asked, "you got yourself a guy?"

"No, no guy yet," she replied, adding a polite smile.

Of course June couldn't let things end there. "Is that because it's harder to find a good Negro man, you know, the marryin' kind?"

"June!" Audrey exclaimed. "Why would you ask such a thing?"

"Well, I don't know," June replied. "I'm just curious."

"That's okay," Nona said. "I don't think it would be any harder than any of you finding a worthy man to marry. I'm just not looking right now, that's all."

A more polite answer than the question deserved. Nona must have felt it was excusable. It wasn't. Not really. That June did not feel the discomfort of her own questions, her own ignorance, was not an excuse. And she was back with more.

"Why are you waiting then?" She asked. "These are a woman's best years."

"I figure," Nona replied, "I'm going to have good years up until the day I die. And if he is to be, he will be waiting for me after I finish my degree and start teaching." She met their eyes, each in turn, and added, "That's my plan."

There was an unusual silence at the table, a vacuum within the constants of plant noise and the distant revving of engines being tested. No one responded until the least likely among them spoke.

"That's a w-w-wonderful p-p-plan."

Chapter 12

It happened as Nurse Lillian said it would, just as Susan had confirmed. The lightening as the baby moved lower allowed Ruth to breathe easier than she had in months. She felt the release of the plug and the trickle of warm fluid, and the discomfort increased—loose bowels, the pain of contractions growing stronger, gripping her closer and closer in time.

And there was no empathy or reassurance from Mrs. Stranton. Whether it was out of a personal sense of condemnation or a dutiful enforcement of society's morals, she offered only her disgust. And Ruth took it. She let the words have their final sting because it would be over soon. She tried hard to believe that.

If it had been up to Mrs. Stranton, Ruth would have suffered unbearable pain in childbirth without relief from drugs as part of her punishment, but it wasn't up to her.

They had shuttled Ruth in through the back door of the hospital and it wasn't until she saw Nurse Lillian's face, the reassuring smile and the promise squeezed around her hand, that she knew that for sure.

All through the remaining hours of labor, Lillian was there, explaining what was happening, giving encouragement. Over and over, "You're doing fine. Everything's perfect. It won't be long." She held Ruth's hand and wiped her face and neck with a cool cloth.

Then, so quickly, it seemed, huge relief, a baby's cry and the attending nurse rushing from the room. Another nurse worked behind sheet-draped knees, and Ruth could see nothing. Lillian remained at the side of the bed, holding Ruth's hand in both of her own. "It's all over, honey," she said with a smile. "It's all over now."

Slow and breathy, Ruth asked, "Can I hold the baby?"

"I'm sorry," Lillian said, pushing wet strands of hair off Ruth's forehead.

"Is it a boy like I thought? Can I just see him? I need to touch him. Please, just let me touch him."

"No, Ruth, I'm sorry," Lillian said. She turned her head in the direction of the other nurse, busy cleaning Ruth, and motioned with her eyes.

She knew this would happen, knew not to ask, but there was a sense of urgency that she didn't expect—to touch him, claim him, save that part of herself. "Please," she pleaded. If not now, then never. Part of her, part of who she was, never known, never touched, never loved—not by her. Her chance gone in a matter of minutes. "Please," she said again, her eyes locked and pleading with Lillian.

"Ruth, it's normal for you to feel like this, but you made the right decision."

Yes, she had signed the papers, made the decision. She knew in her mind that it was best. But it wasn't right. No woman should have to give away her child. In Ruth's heart it would never be right.

She blinked the pleading from her eyes, let them fill and spill over with tears. There was nothing else to do—only cry, only grieve. The tears came heavy now. The sobbing, gentle heaves of her chest at first, now challenged her breath. "What have I done?" she forced through the sobs. "What have I done?"

Lillian leaned down and wrapped her arms around Ruth's head and shoulders. She whispered next to her ear, "You've given your little boy the best chance at a good life that you can give him."

❦ ❦ ❦

Amelia greeted her as expected, eyes wide with apprehension, mouth drawn in sadness, close to tears. She hugged Ruth in the room that had been a refuge for so many months, just as she had Susan on her last day.

"Did you ask?" she said softly, her head tucked beneath Ruth's chin.

"Yes," Ruth replied, "but there is no room for me to stay longer. Another girl will be here to take my room in a few days."

Amelia squeezed her arms around Ruth's waist. "Once you leave, they won't let me talk to you. Oh, Ruth, I can't do this without you."

"Shhh, yes you can," she said, stroking the silky blond hair. "There are a lot of things that you can't do, that *I* can't do—but this you can do. I promise you, you can."

"Was it like Susan said?"

She'd asked herself the same question many times as the day had gotten closer and her own anxiety had increased. Had Susan made it sound easier, less painful, less of an emotional turmoil in order to make them less afraid? Or, had her tolerance to pain been naturally higher, her ability to believe in her choice stronger? Would what was true for Susan be the same for Ruth? Or Amelia? What would be true for them?

Ruth pulled back enough to lift Amelia's chin and look directly into her eyes. "Nurse Lillian was there the whole time just as she said she'd be. And she'll be right there for you, too."

"So what Mrs. Stranton says isn't true? That the pain will make me want to die?"

"They gave both Susan and me something to help with the pain, and they will you, too. Lillian will make sure of it." The other pain, the emotional torture, Ruth wasn't sure needed to be shared. Maybe it was only her own private torture, something in her that couldn't accept, that refused the logic which kept her connected to a part of her she would never know. Maybe Amelia wouldn't be tortured in the same way. Maybe fear of going home to a familiar danger would be the torture for her, rather than giving up her baby. Maybe she would face both.

Ruth tightened her arms around Amelia as she once again nestled her head beneath Ruth's chin. "I talked with Nurse Lillian," Ruth said, and quickly added, "I didn't tell her what happened to you, only that you count on me and that I take that seriously. It's up to you to tell her what you want her to know. But she has been true to her word and you can trust her." She felt Amelia nod against her chest. "I asked her to help us write to each other while you are here and she said she would. You need to give her your letters tucked inside your spiral notebook and she'll send them to me. I'll send my letters to her house and she will put them in the notebook and give it back to you. I'll give you my notebook so that you'll always have one and no one will know the difference."

"Where will you go?"

"Nurse Lillian's mother-in-law found a place for me to rent."

"Is it close by? Maybe they will let you visit here."

"In Ypsilanti, about thirty miles from here," Ruth replied. "And they're quite strict about visitors, but I'll see." Visiting was out of the question, Ruth knew that, but for now Amelia needed something to hang on to. There was so little that she could give Amelia right now, at least she could give her that.

Ruth broke their embrace. Amelia lifted her head, cheeks wet with tears, but kept her eyes on Ruth. "Tell me what you know for sure," Ruth said, with one last chance to run through their routine of reassurance.

Amelia answered softly, "I know that you care about me."

Ruth waited for what they had practiced many times.

"I know you wouldn't lie to me." Amelia's voice gained strength. "I know this isn't my fault." She wiped her cheeks dry. "And I'm a good person, and I'm smart, and I deserve to be treated with respect."

Ruth grasped the top of Amelia's arms. "And what do you promise me once you are home?"

"That I will be strong and watchful. And I will not be in the same place with him without someone else with me."

"You will insist, no matter what anyone says."

"I will insist," Amelia promised.

"And if *they* refuse, *you* refuse."

"Yes."

Ruth cupped Amelia's cheek with her hand. "I'm so proud of you."

"And you promise that you will not forget about me?"

"I promise," Ruth said. "I will answer every letter without fail. Just make sure that you always get the mail yourself—don't let anyone find out about the letters."

"I won't."

Ruth hugged her one last time and added, "Now it's my turn to be strong. She won't know it, but Mrs. Stranton will be throwing insults at Joan of Arc, who will handily let them bounce off her breastplate."

Chapter 13

Ruth had been watching her for over a month. A natural beauty with eyes that wouldn't let go. A creature of habit, three days a week, same time, same section of the restaurant. Ruth's section, she counted on it. Counted on the diversion, the mystery—*who was she, where was she from?* And counted on the questions to occupy the late-night emptiness after the noise and bustle of the restaurant could no longer help. It was the only thing she had found that kept the pain at bay and replaced the wondering. That insistent wondering of where he was, who was holding her baby—quieting his cries, kissing the downy soft head. Would they love him as if he were their own? Would they know how much a part of her he was, or how much she longed to touch him, smell him, cuddle him against her heart? Would they care? Would they ever tell him that she existed? Even more painful than the questions was knowing that there were no answers. So Ruth let her mystery woman fill the nights with new wonder and, at least for a little while, take away the pain.

Some things she knew. The blue coveralls and the time of day said that she worked the day shift at the bomber plant. But the rest she imagined, each night adding a new possibility to the life of the pretty stranger. One night she was the daughter of a prominent politician, satisfying her civil conscience by working for the war effort. Maybe. Another night she was a devoted wife, doing her part back home while her husband flew bombing missions for the Allies. There was even a night that she imagined her mystery woman as a government implant, reporting directly to the President on the efficiency of the country's largest plant. And last night she had dared to imagine that

81

there was no man at all in her mystery woman's life, and never would be. It was the most intriguing fantasy of them all. Ruth planned on revisiting that one over and over. It made her smile.

"I'll have the chicken à la king special," the mystery woman said, milk chocolate eyes meeting Ruth's and releasing their usual zing of electricity.

"I'm sorry," Ruth replied, "that went really fast today. We are all out."

"Oh," she said, "well, what about the ham and macaroni?"

Ruth smiled and slid her order pad and pencil into the front pocket of her apron. "Let me check first to be sure we have it. The specials have been flyin' out of here." She turned and began to make her way between the tables toward the large, horseshoe-shaped counter in the back.

As she passed a nearby table, a man grasped her arm and stopped her. "Hey, sweet thing," he said with a grin. "I'm starvin'. Don't suppose you got a nice chunk of beef back there for me."

"No, sir, we don't serve rationed beef."

He still gripped her arm. "Well, then, get me a big plate of spaghetti, heavy on the sauce."

When he released her arm, Ruth replied, "As soon as I finish this order, I'll be right with you." She turned away, refusing him further eye contact or the chance to respond.

When she returned she purposely took the long way around the man's table. She smiled at her mystery woman and placed a glass of iced tea on the table. "We do have the ham and macaroni," she said. "Your order—"

"You know, where I come from," the man had turned in his chair to get Ruth's attention, "you serve a man first, and nice women don't wear trousers and work in factories."

The comments stopped Ruth short. She was unprepared to answer him. No one had said anything like that in the months that she'd worked at The Bomber. If anyone else thought the same thing, they had never said it out loud. Working women seemed to be a given. Even the name of the restaurant made it clear that a huge percentage of the clientele worked at the plant.

"I don't know where you are from, sir," Ruth said, trusting her diplomacy, "but this restaurant proudly serves the workers at the Willow Run Plant, both men *and* women. They put in long hours of hard work to provide the military with the planes they need, and when they come here, we take good care of them."

One of the other waitresses had already notified the manager. Jim D., thirties and slender, the sleeves of his white shirt rolled to the elbows, strode calmly to the table. "Ruth," he said with a nod. He extended his hand to the man, older and beefier than himself. "I'm the manager here. Is there something I can help you with?"

The man pushed back hard against the back of the chair, exaggerating the barrel of his chest. "You can start by putting your waitress," he motioned with his thumb toward Ruth, "in her place. You know, treat men with respect, take the order, and keep her mouth shut."

Jim slid his hands into his pockets and cocked his head questioningly at Ruth.

"I explained to him that I was in the middle of taking care of another table and would be right back to get his order."

The man caught Jim's eye and motioned with his thumb to the table behind him. When there was no immediate response, the man added, "A woman factory rat in trousers."

"I understand," Jim began, returning his focus to the man's self-satisfied expression, "that FDR himself is counting on our bomber plant here to give him the majority of B-24s he needs to help win this war. People here take that responsibility seriously. We consider that *our* plane," he said, pointing to the pictures of the planes and crews lining the wall. "And I just learned something the other day. There've been around ten thousand women working in that plant to make that possible." He hesitated a moment. The self-importance had vanished from the man's face. Then Jim added, "My sister works there."

Ruth had suspected it was coming, the shiny bright nail that hammered the man's trousers to his seat, but she still had trouble stifling the smile that begged for expression. She bit her bottom lip and managed to suppress it.

Jim finished with a wink to Ruth. "Ruth is one of our best waitresses. She'll take real good care of you, just as she does all her customers."

Nothing more was said. Nothing was needed. Ruth apologized to her mystery woman for the delay, served her her meal, and took the man's order as if nothing had been said.

The restaurant bustled with dinnertime capacity and Ruth had only brief glimpses at the woman she wished she knew more about. A glance here and there between orders and smiles and balancing plates and refilled drinks to see that she was still there, complementing her dinner with a dose of newspaper news. And then another turn-around to glance, and the woman was gone.

Ruth delivered a tray of balanced plates to another table of plant workers and slipped by the now empty table to collect her always-generous tip. This time it was tucked beneath a folded napkin and it was far beyond generous. A dollar, almost twice what the woman paid for her meal, rested beneath the note written on the back of the receipt.

In pretty, free-looping script were the words, *Thank you. Audrey.*

Tonight her mystery woman had a name.

Chapter 14

She had wished away time before. The days at the Crittenton Home, saturated in anxiety and uncertainty, had seemed so much longer than their true time. And the time now at night, those minutes and hours of guilt and longing Ruth wished could be swept away by sleep. It seemed at times that she was wishing her life away.

These last four days, though, had been wished away with anticipation and an excitement Ruth hadn't felt since Sarah. She hadn't been sure then if what she felt was real, if the sparks of electricity and the desire to share every part of her mind and body with a woman would satisfy the yearning. Or if it should. Her doubt was costly, painful—to herself and Paul and to a son she would never know. All because she doubted, because she was afraid.

But she knew now. Even if her mystery woman had only been a diversion, a fun fantasy each night that took her away from the pain and kept the tears at bay. Even if that's all she would ever be, the past few days felt like a beginning.

Like every weekend, Ruth had washed and dried and folded Mrs. Welly's laundry and done the weekly housecleaning, right down to dusting the fancy wooden spindles of the stately wooden staircase. Unlike a normal weekend, though, Ruth hadn't noticed her legs aching, right behind her knees, or the consistent pain in her lower back. Nor had she wished that she could lie down after each task, just for fifteen minutes, just to stretch her back and lift her tired legs. Instead her thoughts were on a lovely diversion, on Audrey. Her name was Audrey.

❧ ❧ ❧

The trays had never felt lighter. Ruth carried them, balanced shoulder-high with hot dinners, and glided effortlessly between the tables without bumping a hip against the back of a chair once. Grouchy patrons didn't faze her. Nothing was going to bother her today.

She glanced at the clock on the wall behind the cash register. The first shift from the plant would start filing through the door in just a few minutes. Ruth placed a bill on a table, and smiled and thanked the couple finishing their coffee. As she slipped her order pad back into its pocket, she checked the spot on her blouse still damp from a quick borax scrub to remove a splatter of gravy. Presentable. She wanted to be presentable. It hadn't been something she'd worried much about until today. And why, didn't seem to make much sense— if Audrey hadn't noticed stains, or hair out of place, or a tired expression by now, then she hadn't been looking. Nevertheless, Ruth checked for errant hairs and tucked them neatly behind the hairpin above her ear.

A moment later she turned to see Audrey making her way to a table next to the wall of bomber pictures. She gave herself an extra moment to get past the jump of her heartbeat, but today it refused to settle back down. Giving it more time was out of the question since Audrey had already sent a smile her way. Ruth sucked in a breath, returned the smile, and headed for the table.

She stayed with Audrey's eyes, and kept her voice low. "You shouldn't have left a tip like that."

"I wanted you to know how much I appreciated what you did," Audrey replied.

"But I really didn't do anything."

Audrey leaned forward over the table and matched Ruth's low tone. "You faced down a man who would have had you fired, and you never even blinked."

"But he was wrong," she replied without hesitation.

Audrey's face lit up into a huge smile. "Yes," she said, "he *was* wrong."

People were squeezing behind her and the tables were filling fast. "Okay," Ruth said, pulling her order pad from her apron, "let me take your order and get to work before I *do* get fired."

She tried not to make it obvious, but she watched Audrey closer than usual tonight. Between orders, between serving and refills and questions, she snuck in glances at Audrey's table. This time Ruth would not let her slip out before she had a chance to say more than, *how is your dinner?* Or *can I get you anything else?*

Another glance and Audrey had finished eating. Ruth dropped off a cup of coffee at a table on her way, and placed Audrey's bill next to her cup. "Can I get you another cup of coffee?" she asked, hoping for a few more minutes.

"No, thanks," she replied. "I've noticed since we've been working longer hours and I'm eating so late that I don't sleep as well with more than one cup of coffee."

Where it came from Ruth had no idea, but without planning it she did something that she had never done before. The words just tumbled out. "Would you want to meet me for dessert when I get off work?" There was no immediate shake of her head, only the corners of Audrey's mouth curling into a smile. Ruth continued: "I get off in about thirty minutes, and I have a dollar that's burning a hole in my pocket and screamin' ice cream."

"I love ice cream."

Had she been holding her breath? Seemed like she had been the whole time.

Audrey offered much needed relief. "Do you want to meet at the soda shop just past the bus stop on Michigan?"

"You do know your ice cream," Ruth said and smiled.

"Thirty minutes, then."

৶ ৶ ৶

This was a mistake. She had known it the moment she realized she was purposely choosing a table in Ruth's section, and then again the first time she let her eyes stay too long. Yet, here she sat, waiting for a woman who touched all those nuances, the ones that made it too easy to ignore the consequences. Dangerous in so many ways; she knew that only too well.

The thought, the near decision to leave, came too late. Ruth burst through the door and flashed a smile worthy of the movie screen. It took only that and the desire to know more about this woman to forget about consequences for just a little bit. Just a little ice cream indulgence and a little break from routine. That was all.

"Not to say that The Bomber doesn't have acceptable ice cream," Ruth said as she slid into the booth, "but *this* is killer diller."

"That's because it's the real McCoy. They use real milk and the right amount of sugar."

"A couple of weeks after I got here, some military guys told me about this place."

Audrey nodded. "The government is taking care of their soldiers, and they love their ice cream. It's a 'morale booster'. We're lucky the plant is here."

They ordered their ice cream loaded, and Audrey started the conversation. Somehow asking the questions equated with less need to lie herself. "You said you moved here not long ago. Where are you from?"

"My family is from Indiana," Ruth replied. "I'm from here now. What about you?"

Perfect. She's playing the same game—and well. "Family is from Ohio. I'm from here."

Ruth smiled and seemed content to let Audrey ask questions.

"I don't recall telling you that I would, in fact, rather eat ice cream than breakfast. So *why* did you ask me to come here tonight?"

"A process of elimination," Ruth said with a serious, matter-of-fact look on her face. "I started with the other waitresses. Betsy has three kids and always heads straight home to relieve her mother. Edna has a new boyfriend who she sneaks off to spend time with before she goes home. And Catherine doesn't like ice cream, which makes me worry about her. So," she said, tilting her head and turning the palms of her hands up, "I figured someone coming in regularly, eating alone after work, just might be waiting for someone to eat ice cream with."

Audrey grinned. "You're quite intuitive."

"Oh, you know, it's one of those gifts that God gives to make up for a lack of natural grace." Ruth finally smiled, welcomed the dish of double-dip treat, and raised her spoon over the table to click against Audrey's. "To decadence."

Audrey returned the smile. "No matter how fat it makes us." She enjoyed her treat, something she realized she hadn't done for some time. And more than that, she realized how much she missed having a friend that she could do things like this with. As much as she cherished her friendship with Nona, there was much they couldn't share, and wishing it different would not change it. So, what was wrong with this? she wondered, watching Ruth close her eyes and audibly savor a spoonful of ice cream, chocolate and caramel. What could be so wrong?

Chapter 15

Could she have avoided it a little longer? Ruth stopped at the top of the stairs, changed her mind, and headed back down without changing out of her uniform.

"I'm going to take a walk, Mrs. Welly," she said as she passed through the kitchen.

"Right now? Dinner will be ready soon."

"I won't be long." Enough time to walk through the neighborhood and let tired legs do what they could to clear her mind.

Yes, she could have avoided this for a while longer, not made the call to her mother, not opened herself up to what she knew would come from it. But it was inevitable if she wanted to know where her brother was, how he was, and yes, how Paul was. She cared if they were safe, so the decision and the call had been made and the anticipated insinuations and judgments endured.

It was a quiet neighborhood, far enough away from the center of town to see minimal motor traffic, and far enough from campus to have little foot traffic. The only intrusion was the constant drone of engines overhead as bomber after bomber took its test flight—something that was becoming less noticeable the longer she was here.

She turned the corner, halfway around the block, and waved at the postman across the street delivering from a hefty bag slung over his shoulder. The temptation had been huge to write to her mother instead of call. Easier, Ruth was sure, to write how she felt without having to hear the tone of her mother's responses. But a letter would have disclosed where she was, opened the possibility of an unwelcome visit, from her parents, or even more troubling, eventually from Paul. Her pace slowed to a more casual stroll while her mother's words haunted her. No surprise that the conversation had begun with her mother's undisguised indignation that her daughter had waited this long to contact her family. The call from the Home that she had decided to go elsewhere rather than back home was insulting. The worry she had put them through was inexcusable, the embarrassment intolerable. And the questions and stories that they were forced to field and create—how could she? All this, Ruth admitted, was expected, and deserved, to a certain extent.

Her mother, of course, spoke for her father as well. At least that was the premise. For the embarrassment, probably. The worry—well, Ruth wondered. The truth was that there was little she would ever be able to do to change whatever her parents felt or thought about her, especially now. The decisions she had made for her life were too far outside acceptable bounds and pretense was too exhausting. Distance was the only answer. The farther away she stayed, the easier it would be, for both herself and her parents. And maybe someday it just wouldn't matter.

Gratefully, the rest of the conversation had put her mind at ease. Her brother, at last account, was uninjured and his unit was reinforcing ground forces in Italy. She loved him. The little curly-headed boy with the thumbprint dimple in his chin, the little boy she had doted on as a big sister, had grown into a carbon copy of their father. He was as traditional as she was not, as different from her as he could be, but she loved him. And as relieved as *she* was that he was safe, how much greater must that relief be for her parents. Their concern hinged on every letter they received and they worried whenever the time between letters seemed too long. This was real worry, justified worry. A far cry from worrying about what the world would make of a young woman daring to live her life on her own terms.

Ruth stopped in front of the large gray house with the wraparound porch only three doors down from Mrs. Welly's. She sat on the short brick wall stretching along the walk. Her legs ached. She was tired and struggling to keep frustration from becoming anger.

Her mother had, just as Ruth suspected she would, dismissed her request not to, and had told Paul everything—the sacrifice she had made in order to know that he was all right. Physically, he was. His carrier, the USS *Hornet*, would be headed for the Philippine Sea.

Otherwise, though, he was exactly as she expected him to be after being told that he had fathered a child he would never know. He was devastated. And his response, if truthfully relayed by her mother, fell somewhere between hurt and anger.

"Is this why you broke it off with me? How could you not be honest with me about something so important? How could you give our baby away? All I wanted was a life and a family with you." All those feelings, all that pain was exactly what Ruth had hoped to spare him. And she would have done just that if not for her mother. She could think of no greater disrespect for her wishes, no bigger denial of her right to decide what was right for her life than this betrayal.

For so much of her life she had tried to understand her mother. At first, when Ruth was so young, it was to try to fit what was natural to what her mother taught should be. Shouldn't she question and challenge? It seemed the natural way to learn. Did it come down to what *could* be versus what *should* be? How else did you find what was possible? But she had always seemed to question what she should have accepted and to challenge what was set in stone. And when she was older, she couldn't understand why her mother never allowed herself even a step outside the boundaries; she didn't seem happy in her expected role. What was most difficult to understand, though, was why she wouldn't want her daughter to take the steps that she herself could not. Why wouldn't her mother want her to find the happiness that was missing in her own life?

Ruth had tried, really tried, but now, after this, even understanding wouldn't be enough. There was very little respect, and certainly no trust, left. Her mother could judge and try to create guilt, she could plead, but she would never again be able to affect Ruth's life. That she would guarantee.

Chapter 16

It took weeks for what had happened to be apparent. It had occurred so naturally. The spaces in Audrey's life, vacancies once filled with family and friends and lovers, were occupied now by Ruth. She had walked in and filled them up so naturally that Audrey had taken this long to realize.

They talked of work and fellow workers, of war and worry, and books they'd read. They went to movies, shopped together, and treated themselves to the occasional evening of loaded ice cream. What they did not do was talk of their past, or their futures, or who they really were. And that hadn't escaped the observation of Audrey's best friend.

"Mm, mm, mm," Mrs. Bailey muttered when it was clear that she was bankrupt and that once again Nona had won their Friday night game of Monopoly. She shook her head, looked over her glasses at Audrey and said, "When you gonna finally beat this girl? I'm runnin' quite a dry spell myself."

"I gave it my best," Audrey replied.

Mrs. Bailey pushed her chair back from the dining table and groaned as she rose slowly from her seat. "All right, I'll leave you to deal with the ruler of the world here," she said, placing a kiss on Nona's head and heading for her bedroom.

"Good night, Mrs. Bailey," Audrey said, "sleep well." She gathered the paper money and stacked it neatly in the game box as Nona collected the game pieces.

"I don't know what it was that made Mrs. Bailey like me," Audrey said, "but I'm very glad she does."

"You charmed her," Nona said and smiled.

"Well, not consciously."

Nona folded the board and closed up the box. "See? Just being you can work. I don't think you've told her one lie about yourself."

"I guess because it hasn't been necessary yet."

"And Ruth?" Nona asked. "Have you lied to her?"

The space between Audrey's brows pinched into a tight crease. "Just because I'm clobbered by your accent doesn't make it okay for you to say anything you want, you know."

The corners of Nona's mouth curled slightly. "I can say anything because you trusted me with who you are. That's what makes it okay. Are you going to trust Ruth the same way?"

Audrey slumped back in her chair. "You're safe, Nona."

"Safe." Nona leaned forward and forced eye contact. Her voice was discreetly low. "Because I will always keep your secret."

"And because," her tone matching Nona's, "I don't have to worry that you will have feelings for me that would destroy you. I know how strong your convictions are. You know exactly who you are and what you want for your life."

"You worry that Ruth doesn't?"

"I don't know if she does or not. Sometimes I don't even know what I want for my life."

"So it's possible that you are worrying for no reason. Ruth may know what she wants, and she may just want a casual friend, someone to do things with. Why do you think it could be more than that?"

"Because she's *not* telling me anything, that's how I know." She acknowledged a questioning look from Nona. "Nothing about her life before she came here—nothing about the people in her life, friends or family. The same thing I'm doing."

"You could be wrong. She could be unwilling to share that part of her life for a lot of reasons."

Audrey nodded. "I know that's the logical way to look at it. But there are things that you feel, things that aren't explained logically."

"Do you think you can explain it to the non-logical part of my brain?"

Audrey leaned forward, resting her forearms on the table. "The signals," she began. "The same unspoken signals that I'm sure you must have felt when you knew someone was interested in you—and maybe you found yourself returning the interest. You catch them watching you, too often, too long. And when you catch their eyes you hold them longer than you should."

"You find excuses, not reasons, to be wherever they are," Nona added.

"And you let the physical space dissolve. You let them lean close, you welcome it, look forward to it. And they know it."

Nona nodded. "So Ruth's doing that?"

"And *I'm* doing that," Audrey said. "But I need to stop. I need to let it settle into a friendship, just a friend who I can go places with and do things that you and I can't do together. That's all it can be."

"What will you do if she wants it to go beyond that? You recognize the signals, she must have recognized the same thing from you." Nona waited for a response but there was none. "What then, Audrey?"

"I'll deny it. I'll lie. I've become quite good at it."

"Is that what you are going to do the rest of your life, deny something that might make you happy? What are you going to do, live alone? Marry a man? My father would say that you are whistling past the graveyard."

"I'm not like you, Nona. I don't have a plan. I don't know what my life will be like. All I know is that I need to hang on to the few things I *do* know. For now, that's all I can do."

"So what do you know?"

"That I'm lucky to have a friend like you—one person in my life who knows who I am, one person I don't have to lie to. There are times when I doubt my own ability to be able to tell the lies from the truth."

"The lies you tell to keep your secret safe?"

"No, it's not the lies that I tell others. It's the ones I tell myself. Is it possible that I can be a good person, that I can trust my own decisions, and still lie to the rest of the world?"

"What makes someone good?" Nona asked. "Caring about other people, making sacrifices for others or for your country? Isn't that what you were doing when you spoke up for me when I was late for work, and when you honor the rationing and restrictions without complaining? You measure goodness by what is in your heart."

Who measured that goodness? Had others judged her as Nona had, seen some measure of goodness in her but never said it? It wouldn't be so unexpected since no one else knew her secret. But Nona did, and still she offered a measure Audrey dared not offer herself. She couldn't own it, no matter how much Nona thought she should. "I don't see how that can ever be enough to pay for destroying someone's life. There is nothing I could do now that could pay that debt." She shook her head, a personal emphasis. "Good people forgive, and I can't forgive me."

"You never explained what happened, only that you feel responsible for it."

"I've never put it into words, not even to myself. I can't, Nona, not yet."

"It's all right, you don't have to," Nona replied. "But when you do want to talk about it, I'm here to listen. Whatever it is, though, I'll probably still think you judge yourself too harshly."

"No," Audrey insisted, "it was selfish. I wanted her to love me. I allowed it."

"Do you really *allow* someone to love you? How do you control someone else's feelings? I don't believe you can, Audrey."

"But if I had walked away, if I had told her it was wrong for us."

"Did you think it was?"

Audrey lowered her eyes. "What I thought lost out to what I felt. Society says that it's wrong." She looked again into Nona's eyes. "And the Bible says it's wrong."

"Well, a lot of people believe that the Bible condones slavery, too. It's been used to justify owning slaves here and in Europe. But does that make it right? Audrey, faith is a personal thing. We each need to come to our own understanding of it," Nona said. "For me, I trusted my own reading and the teaching of my pastor, and I believe that Jesus brought a new covenant in the New Testament. The new covenant was love, and new replaces old. I don't see how I can go wrong following that covenant."

"I guess I need to read it for myself, then. Maybe God can forgive me even if I can't." Audrey kept her eyes on Nona's. "But even if there is forgiveness, I know I can never let what happened, happen again. I know the danger now, I know it's real, and I can never forget it."

Chapter 17

The letters were as regular as the sunrise, arriving every Monday and keeping Ruth as much a part of Amelia's life as distance and rules would allow.

Ruth retrieved this week's letter from the lace runner on Mrs. Welly's dining table and headed upstairs to her room. With her landlady away visiting, the evening was her own and Ruth welcomed the solitude.

She quickly shed her uniform and the discomfort of her girdle and hose. With a long sigh she stretched back onto the bed and stared blankly at the ceiling. Lately there was nothing that felt this good. The ache in her legs and lower back soon eased, and Ruth reached blindly for the letter on the bedside stand. She slipped her fingertip under the edge of the flap, slid it open, and lifted the folded notebook pages.

Dear Ruth,

I will never know how to thank you for your friendship. Wherever we end up in our lives I want you to know that I never would have been able to get through this without you.

Nurse Lillian thinks that I will deliver in just over four weeks from today. She said she will be right beside me just as you said. I have kept your letters hidden in the lining of my suitcase and take them out to read at night when I am most afraid. Your words give me strength because I know you believe me.

I am not afraid of the pain now, I believe you and Nurse Lillian. But what will happen to my heart? I feel this baby's every move, when it stretches and pushes. I know when it's awake and sing my favorite songs for it to sleep at night. Will I know if it's a boy or a girl, or what color its hair is or its eyes? What will I do with the emptiness it will leave behind?

But what I am most afraid of is going home. My father warned me that I had better learn this lesson and become the good girl that he can be proud of. What if it's not possible? I would rather stay here. I'm getting used to Mrs. Stranton. She thinks if everyone follows the rules, here and when we all go home, that we will have happy lives.

I know she blames us girls for making mistakes, but Nurse Lillian says that it's her way of saying that girls do have control over what their lives will be like. I wish she knew what happened to me, but I don't think she would believe me either. If I could just stay here and let her think that I need more lessons and that I really want to know how to make my life better. She knows that I work hard at my duties, and I could help more if I could stay. I do feel safe here. Maybe if Nurse Lillian could talk to her.

I hope you are happy where you are. I wish I could be like you and make my own money and decide where I want to live. I miss you terribly. I am waiting for your next letter, and trying to be strong.

Your friend,

Amelia

It wasn't as though she hadn't thought about the day Amelia would have to go home. The thought, the worry of it, had invaded Ruth's days more and more as the weeks went by. And the last letter from Susan was no help. The timing of her marriage and honeymoon made it strikingly clear that the responsibility for Amelia was now solely Ruth's. Whatever plan she'd hoped the two of them would come up with to help Amelia was gone. So what now? Support her, advise her from a distance. She was so young, and frightened and alone. She'd get through the delivery, she'd face the doubts, and the guilt, and even the emptiness of giving up her baby. Ruth could share that much with her, and cry the tears they would both shed. But she couldn't protect her. And the anxiety that was coursing through Ruth right now drove its message home—there was *no* one to protect her.

A surge of panic brought Ruth upright. Perspiration covered her body. She grabbed quick breaths as her thoughts scrambled for a way. There had to be something she could do. She rose from the bed, paced barefoot across the cool wooden floor. Across to the window and back. On her third trip to the window, Ruth stopped. She stared blankly at the familiar patch of yard, and then she knew.

Quickly she dressed, grabbed the letter and her house key, and hurried down the stairs.

೫ ೫ ೫

There were a number of ways to describe nights like this—relaxing, rejuvenating, essential. They were all of that for Audrey. They gave her time away from the rest of her life. Alone time, selfish time. Much needed time. Especially tonight.

She had already moved her bed to the other side of the room, against the wall of her night-shift neighbor and away from the grizzly snore of the neighbor on day shift. She had stripped and showered, donned a thin cotton nightgown, and nestled into the corner of her bed to listen to the radio. A reporter would tell her how they were winning the battles and calm her worries, and Fibber would make her laugh by lying to Molly. She would rest and sleep early and, at least for a while, not think about Ruth. There would be no guarding her words to Ruth, no confessions needed to Nona. Her heart would settle, her senses clear. And here in her little space, she would control her world. Yes, that was the plan, and it was a good one.

Then came a knock on her door. She overrode the fleeting temptation not to answer it. But the light was on, and she was clearly home. It would be beyond rude. Reluctantly, Audrey pulled on the robe draped over the foot of the bed, and went to the door.

"Who is it?" she called.

"Audrey, it's me, Ruth."

The sound of her voice did exactly what tonight was supposed to avoid. Her heartbeat sprinted ahead on its own, her thoughts

103

lost direction. A smile took over reason and Audrey opened the door.

"Oh, Audrey, I'm sorry. You're ready for bed. I don't—"

"No, no. Come in." The look in Ruth's eyes justified disturbing even a rare deep sleep. "What is it, Ruth? Is something wrong?"

"There's no one else I trust," she said, stepping into the room. "I need to talk to someone."

"Here," Audrey said, pulling the chair away from the table, "sit down and I'll get us something to drink." She clicked off the radio beside the bed and fetched Cokes from the icebox.

"I hope this isn't expecting too much of our friendship," Ruth began. "I can't go to my family and I don't know anyone else here like I do you."

"Of course you can talk to me. What is it?"

Ruth offered a relieved sigh. "I'm not sure where to begin, or how much would be more than you would want to know. All the way over here I thought about how I should explain. I can't ask for advice unless you know the whole situation, so I hope you will understand."

Ruth's apprehension was apparent. And if Audrey was right about why, she couldn't even reassure her that she would indeed understand. She couldn't tell Ruth that she knew what she was afraid to say. It would only expose her own secret, and worse, her own feelings. She couldn't chance what she might see in Ruth's eyes or hear in her voice that could end in her pulling Ruth to her side and lead to an embrace that shouldn't happen, couldn't happen. She remained silent, waited for Ruth's courage to win out, and vowed denial.

"I need your advice and maybe your help if you are willing," Ruth said. "I have a young friend who is in trouble."

Audrey released a long exhale as a wave of relief eased away the tension. Silence, she was grateful for her own silence. "I hope I can help."

"I do, too," Ruth said. "She's really got no one but me, and I have no idea what to do." She leaned forward heavily, her forearms on the table. "Her name is Amelia. She just turned fifteen. Her family sent her away to a home for unwed mothers." Ruth hesitated and dropped her head for a moment. When she looked up again, the tentativeness was gone. There was directness in her eyes and firmness in her voice.

"Her uncle did that to her and no one will believe her. The Home will send her right back home, right back where it can keep happening." She handed Audrey the letter she had been gripping tightly. "She's so scared, Audrey."

Audrey read the letter quickly. Ruth's intensity, as compelling as it was, wasn't necessary. Amelia's words, the simple beseeching, was all she needed. "Where is home for Amelia?"

"Ohio," Ruth replied.

"So far away. And I think you are right, she is in danger when she goes back."

"I tried to prepare her the best I could. I told her to never be in the same room alone with him, and to always be aware of where he is."

"Do you think her parents have reason not to believe her?" Audrey asked.

"No. I think they just won't believe her, just don't want to believe her."

Audrey returned the letter to Ruth. "Does she have other family she can go to?"

"She said no, but I wonder if it's because she's too shy or maybe too afraid to ask."

"So she will be sent back home and you plan to help her through letters."

Ruth nodded. "I told her that she has to watch for the mail each day and once she reads my letters to burn them. I wouldn't want the letters to agitate the situation. But I'm thinking that it won't be enough, not after this letter." She held Audrey's gaze and asked, "He'll try to do it again, won't he?"

Her answer, "Yes, probably," held little effect except to reinforce Ruth's fear. Instead she asked, "What do you know about him?"

"Only what I could pull out of her about how it all started. He's her father's brother and lives next door. He's not married, so Amelia's duties are to clean house for him and do his laundry on Saturdays. When his work schedule changed and he didn't work Saturdays anymore, she found herself alone in the house with him."

"How long has it been going on?"

"Since she was eleven."

Audrey tipped her head back and closed her eyes for a moment. "This is making me sick to my stomach. What the hell does a man tell a little girl to justify that?"

"That she's his special girl. That he's teaching her how a man should love her." Ruth's tone sharpened. "No one *teaches* how to love. I told her that. And that what he did to her had nothing to do with love. Nothing."

Ruth was angry. Clearly and righteously angry. And fearful. Audrey could sense it, from the quiver she heard beneath the force of her words, and the moisture threatening the corners of Ruth's eyes. Fearful of letting down someone who was depending on her. "How can I help?" Audrey asked.

"I don't know. I want to think that there is something, and that I just haven't found it yet. If you have *any* ideas," her eyes searched Audrey's, waiting, hoping.

"We know you can continue the letters while she's in the Home, right?"

"As long as no one finds out. Nurse Lillian sneaks my letters in and Amelia's out. The rules of the Home are very strict. No contact with anyone outside during the whole time the girls are there. They can't leave the grounds—no walks, or visits, or shopping—except for the times that Nurse Lillian is able to get permission for them to go to her home on holidays or special occasions." Audrey didn't have the whole picture yet, and that was fine. There wasn't time for complications, only solutions. They needed to slow down the panic of time passing and concentrate on what was most important and probable.

"Then you need to use those letters," Audrey was saying, "to give Amelia the strength of Samson and the resolve of Moses."

Ruth stared blankly somewhere past Audrey's shoulder. Slowly, as if she was answering an unspoken question, she shook her head. "What do I say? What makes you think I can make that kind of difference?"

"The part of you that spoke out against the man in The Bomber. You didn't hesitate or apologize, you just said what you believed. It was an unselfish thing to do." Audrey locked her eyes onto Ruth's.

"Can you put into words what gives *you* that kind of confidence?" The answer that Audrey wanted for herself ever since that day in the restaurant. It was what made this woman different—that she was so sure, so confident—and the very thing that made her so dangerous. But now the answer had a reason beyond herself, her own selfish curiosity, a reason bigger and much more important.

"Right now?" Ruth asked. "I don't think I could think my way through a letter right now."

"No, don't worry about the letter. Tell *me* how Ruth Evans became a waitress, living on her own, with the conviction of a Suffragette."

Ruth hesitated, introspective, before she answered. "How did I become who I am," she said, with the beginning of a frown. "I had no plan to be where I am, who I am. I had a lot of questions. But instead of answers I got expectations—other people's expectations of who I was and what my life should be. I was meant to do what they expected. And I tried to be that person. But you know what I found out? That I *couldn't* be that person." As Ruth continued to talk, Audrey pulled a pad of paper from a drawer on her side of the table. "I'm not meant to be a waitress, either, or any one thing." Audrey was writing. "No one else is going to decide that for me, I won't allow it. Months ago I wrote the letter that I had to write to tell my family just that—that their restrictions, their limitations, their expectations no longer apply to me. *I* will decide where I should live, how I should live—and who I should love. *I* will make those decisions. I'll make my own mistakes and let them make me stronger. *I* get to decide who I am." She took a deep breath and stared intensely at Audrey. "What are you writing?"

"The best testament I've ever heard." She looked up to meet Ruth's eyes. "You are amazing. Whatever made you doubt your ability to help Amelia believe in herself?"

"I'm sure you wouldn't think me amazing if you knew of the mistakes I've made and the pain they have caused others. I'm far from amazing, I only hope that what I've learned can help someone like Amelia."

"You will," Audrey said, pushing the paper across the table, "this will. Write the letter. Write as many as it takes. Start with your own strength, and counter each of her fears with something you know is sure and proven."

"Is it wrong of me to be glad that I disrupted your evening?"

Audrey smiled. "Well, now I have a friend with no shame."

Ruth finally smiled back. "Yes, I'm afraid you do." She folded Audrey's paper together with Amelia's letter and rose from the table. "But I do have a smidgeon of manners, enough to let you get to bed at a reasonable hour." She checked her watch. "And if I hurry I'll be able to catch the next bus."

"Wait," Audrey said, jumping to her feet. "It'll only take me a minute to dress. I'll walk you to the bus."

"And destroy this image of a hard-boiled apron who defiantly walks the streets alone? Oh, no. It has taken me months to earn that image, and I'm rather proud of it."

They stood at the door as Audrey replied. "I think you have a ways to go before you match my trouser-wearing, wage-earning, family-destroying image." She added a grin. "I will admit, though, that mine came rather easily. The company Star Man made that clear the first day I started work at the plant. Not everyone is happy about women being so independent."

"Well, I for one am through worrying about what they think. It's caused me too much heartache."

"I know about heartache," Audrey returned. "I know it all too well. So if I can help you help someone else avoid it, I'll be happy to."

"It might be more than that," Ruth said, stepping toward Audrey and reaching to close her arms around her. "We might be saving a life. Thank you," she said softly as she released her embrace.

Audrey nodded, and asked the question that she had promised herself not to ask. "Will I see you tomorrow?"

"It's our ice cream day, isn't it? And I'll show you my letter before I send it."

The door closed on the smile that would keep her awake tonight. For moments after Ruth left, Audrey could still feel the arms around her, the crispness of the starched white blouse pressing against the soft cotton of her nightgown. The scent of Ruth lingered in the air.

Avoiding heartache, so easily said, she thought. Was it even possible? Could she, or they, save another from it when they hadn't been able to do it for themselves? Did she dare think she could save another when she had already been responsible for such a horrible loss? If Nona's God was truly a loving God, maybe this was her chance for redemption. Help save a life for one that was lost. She wanted to believe it was possible. She wanted to believe it longer than just tonight.

Chapter 18

"If we weren't on our feet all day long and working as hard as we do," Audrey said between savored spoonsful of ice cream, "we wouldn't dare gorge ourselves like this. We would have to discipline ourselves to once a month and a single scoop with a dribble of chocolate on top. But," she said, raising her eyebrows, "luckily for us, we *do* work that hard."

Ruth dropped her gaze to her nearly empty dish. "I'm already tempting the girlish figure that it took me months to regain."

Audrey let the remark pass without reply, without question. She had decided when the connection to Amelia had first allowed an assumption that it wasn't her question to ask. She finished her last bite of ice cream.

"Before you read my letter to Amelia," Ruth continued, and pulled an envelope from her purse. This time she spoke while looking directly into Audrey's eyes. "You know why I was at the Home with Amelia, don't you?"

"I've learned that's it's better not to make assumptions. Things aren't always what they seem to be."

"Well, if you had assumed that I had been working there, or that my mother or sister worked there, you would have been wrong. I was there for the same reason as Amelia. But, unlike her, it was because of my own mistake, one of a number of mistakes. I have no business asking you for your help, or for your friendship, if you don't really know me. I've hidden things about myself for too long. It has caused too much heartache, and when I left the Home and started fresh I vowed that I would never again do that to people I care about."

It was heartfelt. Audrey saw it in her eyes, a confession long in coming, an honor saved for now. Audrey's honor—to hear it first, right here, tucked in the corner of a soda shop, spoken quietly over ice cream.

She answered the doubt punctuating Ruth's words. "You don't have to worry. If making mistakes changed how I felt about our friendship, I'd be the biggest hypocrite in the world."

But the doubt was still there. "I think we need to talk about them," Ruth said. "At least I do."

Not hard to do, Audrey thought, to listen, to let her say what she hadn't been able to until now. A lot harder might be Ruth hearing the horror of a mistake that Audrey couldn't forgive herself for. There was one way to know, and it *was* inevitable, wasn't it? Sharing, chancing, accepting—or not. At least temptation, the niggling *what if* that had refused to go away, was no longer a concern. Ruth would not be a threat to her resolve not to ruin another lover's life. Instead, Ruth would be another friend like Nona, there for the time most needed to be each other's support and confidant, there until their lives changed. When Nona and Ruth found the men that they would share the intimacies of marriage with, Audrey would bless them and miss them. And in a strange way that was a great relief.

"Then we'll talk about mistakes," Audrey replied. "But not here. Come on, let's walk down by the river."

৩ ৩ ৩

The new spring grass blanketed the stretch of park that hugged the edge of the river as it wound its way through the center of town. The early evening air smelled of dampened earth and sweet, wet grass, settled over the low murmur of slow-moving water and soothed away the tensions of the day.

"I don't want to get this wrong, Audrey. Mistakes rarely hurt only the person making them. I know that from experience. I don't want to do something that makes things worse for Amelia." They settled on a wooden park bench as the sun rested temporarily on the treetops. "That's why I'm so grateful for your help."

"Honestly, Ruth, I may not have any solution, either. And I've made serious mistakes of my own. To do nothing, though, letting status quo be the rule just because an alternative isn't easy, might be the biggest mistake."

Ruth watched the flickers of gold and orange dance across the surface of the water as she spoke. "I've made that mistake. I knew what was accepted and what was expected by my family and my friends. I knew what my life was supposed to be like." She left the dancing flickers and met Audrey's waiting eyes. "And I knew that wasn't who I was. At least, I thought I knew. I don't know now if I was doubting as much as I was wishing. Being someone else was easier than being me."

The relief Audrey was sure she had found was quickly disappearing. With each word, with every second Ruth's eyes held her own, the initial nuances and signals that Audrey had sensed grew more and more valid. More worrisome than that, though, was that she didn't want her to stop. She *wanted* to know who Ruth was.

"I don't know exactly why," Ruth continued, "maybe your confidence, or, I don't know, a lot of little things that made me feel like you'll be okay with who I am. I don't want to lie to you, Audrey, or *let* you think that I'm someone I'm not."

There of course was no other answer. "I will be fine with who you are." *It's myself I'm not fine with.*

"I hurt someone that I cared a lot about because I was trying to be someone else," Ruth explained. "His name is Paul, and he was my best friend. I loved his sweet temperament and the way he smiled at things that delighted me. I loved how considerate of me he was. He'd sacrifice his jacket if he thought I was cold and tell silly jokes when I was sad. I loved so much about him, enough to believe it could change me. Enough to let him believe that I loved him and to let him make love to me before he went overseas. I knew he loved me and I knew how afraid he was to leave. He tried to pretend that he wasn't, but I could tell. He wanted me to know how much he loved me—just in case he didn't come home. I knew. But it didn't change who I am. Having a baby changed me, but not in the way I once hoped."

There was a softening in Ruth's eyes, a distant lingering on a past that was just that. Maybe a cleansing, Audrey thought, a much needed cleansing for the heart. She watched the distance fade.

"I may not have to say this," Ruth said. "I don't know. I've never done this before. But I want you to know that what I've already said will probably be the easiest part to accept."

"You don't have to warn me, Ruth. I'll be fine." Warning wasn't needed, or useful; it couldn't do anything to ease the turmoil that what she already knew was about to unleash. All that was left now was to face it.

"What none of that changed," she said, looking intensely into Audrey's eyes, "is that I couldn't love Paul, as good and sweet a man as he is, like I would love a woman."

Validated now. Said out loud. No chances left for Audrey to convince herself otherwise.

"You know what I mean, don't you?" Ruth asked. "The intimate love that seeps so deep into your being that you can't imagine a moment without it, can't imagine a breath without its strength."

Yes, she knew. The words sparked and flashed through her, bringing back that first purity, bright and true. Breathless honesty that named itself with the first touch of Velma's lips.

"Have you felt that, too?" Ruth asked.

"Yes," she replied and closed her eyes. "Yes." When she looked again, the relief on Ruth's face made it easy to keep the focus off herself. "What happened to that love?" Audrey asked.

"It wasn't for her what it was for me. And it took too long to find that out. She was everything I admired, everything I wanted to be. I didn't want anything else, anyone else from that first time I saw her greeting customers at her father's business. She was confident and funny, and people loved being around her. I loved how she could talk about so many things; she spoke her mind on politics and the war in Europe, and she knew the batting averages of the best hitters in baseball. I wanted to spend every day with her, and it seemed that she wanted to spend that time with me. . . . Then she loved me. And I didn't care what anyone thought. I didn't care what was supposed to be. Nothing else, no one else mattered—only our love for each other." The space between Ruth's brows pressed into a deep crease. "I didn't realize until afterward that she had never said forever. *She never meant forever.*"

Forever. The word hung in the silence between them. It seemed to dare dismissal. Something that until now had not been a conscious thought. It would be now—troubling, improbable, and conscious. "Do you think she was afraid that someone would find out? She could have been afraid of what would happen if they did."

"If she was," Ruth replied, "I never knew it. One night we were having dinner at a restaurant, and a friend who was going to join us cancelled. We were just talking casually about what our day had been like and then, just as casually, she said that she was going to start seeing some man. I couldn't believe what I was hearing. I sat there not knowing what to say for I don't know how long. I was light-headed and felt like I was going to throw up. Finally I asked, 'What about us?' And do you know what she said? What we had been doing was just preparation for marriage. In that moment everything I thought I knew about my life dissolved. My legs were so weak I didn't think I could stand, but I did, and I left her there—and never looked back."

"But you have."

"I didn't realize at the time that that's what I was doing." Her slow nod seemed introspective. "But, yes—when I lied to Paul and said that I loved him and I knew it didn't mean what he wanted it to mean." She turned her focus across the river. The sun had become an orange filigree behind branches of maple and pine. "And again when I realized that my baby would never know me." Her eyes came back to Audrey's. "I decided that even if there is never another woman to love in my life, I will not live my life the way someone else wants me to live it—not my family, or the church, or Mr. or Mrs. No-name passing me on the street. They don't have to be me. They don't have to know what I know or what I feel. I'm not going to live for them and I'll pay no more of their consequences."

Audrey stared, allowed the seconds to stand undisturbed. Ruth made no attempt to pull her eyes away. There wasn't so much as a blink to soften their message, solid, unwavering. "You," Audrey said, "are one of the strongest women I've ever met."

"Me? No. You think it's strength? I don't feel strong as much as I feel angry. And I can't even put that anger on any one thing. Sometimes I just feel angry at the world. But then I muffle it down and move along."

"Until it pushes its way back out," Audrey said, "at things that don't seem at all fair. Maybe it doesn't matter where strength comes from—like good hardened steel coming from a hot furnace. I always thought anger was energy wasted. My father, always the philosopher, claims that anger uses up valuable energy and keeps you from focusing on solutions. And, of course, believes that outward displays of anger are unbecoming of a woman. I grew up believing he was right." With a tilt of her head, Audrey added, "I think you use your anger quite effectively . . . I admire that."

"So what do you do with *your* anger?"

It seemed an odd question at first, or maybe it was just challenging. It made her think back years, identifying an anger that she claimed and expressed without reserve. So long ago, and now so irrelevant in comparison. Being so angry at George, the Saint Bernard who trampled her favorite flower bed, that the whole neighborhood heard her unladylike language as she chased him home. And the time she tried to beat the crap out of the preacher's son after he missed her eye by a fraction of an inch with a BB gun. But past her twelfth birthday she couldn't say the last time she felt that kind of anger. She could remember fear, anxiety, hiding who she was from everyone—hiding who *they* were, worrying that the two of them would be found out. And guilt, oh yes, she felt that, every day, every night for two years now. But anger, where *was* the anger? It was there, tightly bound and silent, but it was there. It was clamped down tight when Velma was taken, held in check with the hope that Audrey was wrong, with the hope that recovery was possible. And it was anger that simmered in her gut at how Nona was treated. "My expressing anger isn't going to change anything."

"Should I believe that?" Ruth asked.

Audrey nodded. "You should help me find out why I believe it." She checked her watch. "But not tonight. We need to catch the last bus before dark."

Chapter 19

"What has you so distracted?" Nona asked as she folded the Monopoly board. "You let Mrs. Bailey almost single-handedly take you out of the game. I knew you were in a different world when she prattled on about bringing your future children here for her to dote on and you were just noddin' your head. Poor sweet woman wants grandchildren so badly. Her daughter's taking her time, and I already told her that I'm not getting married until I have a career."

Audrey smiled. "How could I dash her hopes, as remote as they are, when she's saying things like 'It doesn't matter what color a baby's cheeks are, they all kiss just as sweet'?"

"Uh, huh." Nona pushed the game box to the center of the table and leaned back in her chair to look at Audrey. "Are you going to tell me what's bothering you?"

"I don't know, Nona." Audrey leaned folded arms on the table. "I'm still trying to sort it out myself."

"Maybe I can help."

"I feel like I'm always bringing my troubles to you."

Nona shook her head. "I'm your friend, not just someone you spend evenings with playing board games. And what kind of trouble did I bring you when I was late to work? Only a real friend would have done what you did. I want to be that friend for you, too."

"Sort with me, then," Audrey replied. "It's all connected to Ruth. I have to figure out if there's a way I can help or if I should stay out of things. And either way I'm worried about what it's doing to Ruth."

"Start with what she needs your help with."

"A young girl," Audrey began, and proceeded to give Nona all she knew of the situation. Just repeating the details, and seeing the words reflected in Nona's expression, emphasized the gravity of it for Audrey.

This was more than a problem that Ruth, or anyone, could solve. And that brought Audrey to the other part of her dilemma.

"What worries me just as much, maybe more, is what this whole thing could do to Ruth. She's been through some tough times of her own and I don't know if she has had time to heal, or even to deal with her own issues."

"Does she talk to you about it?"

Audrey shook her head. "She hasn't said that much. All her concentration seems to be on Amelia. And I don't know if it's my place to press her on something so personal."

"Have you confided in her about your own struggle?" Nona asked.

Audrey locked into the dark brown gaze and read the message perfectly. Her response was a thin smile.

"It could be," Nona added, "that trusting you with Amelia's situation is safer for her than trusting you with her own."

"Or dealing with someone else's struggle is easier than dealing with her own."

"Whatever the cause or reason," Nona said, "she is not ready to tell you how or if she is handling her own struggle."

"So would it be wrong of me to bring it up? What if she thinks that she would be burdening me, or—"

"Or maybe since Amelia's problems are more urgent, they *should* rightfully take precedent. I think you are worrying too much, too soon."

"I hope you're right."

"Look, you confided in me when you were ready. You'll confide in Ruth when you're ready. It helps you to be able to voice it, unload it, and feel supported. But not everyone handles it the same way. She may keep it all inside until she sorts it out for herself."

"But what if it festers inside her until it threatens to destroy her, like it has me? I still hurt, and I don't want her to hurt like that."

"Then you'll be there when she needs you, just as I am for you. Find a way to let her know that."

Audrey nodded, her thoughts circling back. "Regardless, Ruth is going to try to help Amelia, there's no question that she'll try. So how am I going to help her, Nona? How do you protect someone when there's no legal way to right a wrong?"

"You said that there is no place for her to go?"

Audrey shook her head. "No family. They don't believe her about her uncle. I wondered about a church. A church helped you when you needed a safe place to stay. But if they knew that she was an unwed mother . . ."

"I wouldn't speak for the white churches, but Negro churches aren't exempt from hypocrisy. There isn't much space between religious and social mores."

"So who's there for someone like Amelia?"

"People who think for themselves, people who decide what is right and wrong in their own hearts. The same kind of people who marched and spoke out in public and risked going to jail and worse so that women could vote. That's who," Nona said. "People like you."

"Me," Audrey echoed. "Me and Ruth. With no time for marching or changing minds, and no plan."

"Then make a plan."

Audrey's voice lacked its usual patience. "Nona, that's what we're struggling with. It seems impossible."

"Have you ever heard of a woman called Moses?"

"A woman?" Audrey shook her head. "No."

"She was a tiny Negro woman who, from all outward appearances, should never have accomplished what she did."

"Which was?"

"Guiding slaves to safety through the Underground Railroad."

"Mrs. Tubman," Audrey declared.

"You *do* know about her."

"I think we lived in one of those houses. My father figured it out when one time he caught me sneaking into the best hiding place ever. I would disappear every time my parents' friends came over with their obnoxious son. My father followed me down into the basement and saw me closing the cupboard door behind me. When he opened it up I wasn't in the cupboard, and he started pounding on the back of it until he got it to open. I was just climbing out of the window well when he caught me."

"I've heard about hidden staircases and tunnels. I love to learn about the different ways they were hidden."

119

Audrey continued. "That was the one good thing that came out of losing my best hiding place. My father explained that the escaped slaves would run to the house, drop down into the window well, crawl through the hidden door, and wait in the cupboard until someone came down to open it. They would get something to eat and clean clothes and then, when it was safe, they would move on."

"To the next station. I wonder if Moses was a conductor to your home. She might have been, you know."

"I don't think so. My father said that she brought slaves through Ohio and all the way into Canada."

"Do you think your father would have been an abolitionist back then?"

"I *don't* know. When he was telling me about the hiding place, it was as if he was teaching one of his classes. It didn't seem personal at all. It seemed like he was talking about someone else's house."

"We don't always know. Sometimes you don't hear what's in someone's heart, but you can see it. A lot of those who participated weren't known abolitionists. That's what made them so effective; no one suspected them." Nona hesitated before adding. "Maybe that's you."

"Going beyond just being encouraging, you mean?"

"Amelia's situation is serious. How committed are you to helping her?"

Audrey frowned. "Ruth's waiting for another letter from her and then we will know more. But Amelia isn't allowed to communicate with her family, so I don't see how anything could have changed. It comes back to us, then—the responsibility, if we're going to take it."

Nona patted her hand over her heart. "Can you not?" she asked.

Chapter 20

A week later Audrey found a place for her anger, a place where it might actually do some good. She had kept her anger bound, denied it a voice, and instead had let guilt have its reign. She'd owned the guilt as she thought she should, and allowed it to shape the possibilities for her life. But what she was going to learn today was about to change that.

For the first time since she'd left her parents' home, the week had included not one evening that she could call her own. She could no longer claim lonely, her evenings were filled with Nona and game night with Mrs. Bailey, and babysitting for Jack and Lucy, and now Ruth. Even today, which she might have spent alone, would belong to Ruth. And that was fine.

Audrey hauled the laundry basket into her room and pushed the door shut with her hip. She dropped the basket below the dried laundry hanging on the clothesline stretched between the bathroom door and the hook on the opposite wall. As quickly as she could, she pulled dry underwear, blouses, and trousers from the line, tossed them on the bed, and hung the wet sheet from the basket in their place.

The expected knock at the door came before she could finish folding the laundry on the bed. She ducked under the sheet, greeted Ruth at the door, and ushered her under the corner of the wet sheet. "Now I should have warned you," she began, "that the excitement happening here on Saturdays might be too much for you."

Ruth offered a weak attempt at a smile and sat tentatively on the edge of a chair.

"You got a letter," Audrey surmised.

"Two," Ruth replied, placing an envelope on the table and sliding it across to Audrey.

Light conversation was out of the question. Audrey opened the letter and read quickly through the gratitude she expected, in search of what was concerning Ruth.

She was sure that she had found it when the sweetness of a child's voice took on a palpable fear.

> *I did as you asked, Ruth, and talked to Nurse Lillian. I told her everything and I could tell from her eyes that she is worried. She tried to make me feel better by telling me how much I have grown and matured since she first met me. But I'm not strong, not like you want me to be. I'm scared, Ruth, I'm so scared. I can't go back home. Please let me come and stay with you. I will work very hard. Maybe someone will want me to clean their house for them. I will make my own money and I will help you all I can. Please, Ruth, don't let them send me back there.*

Audrey met the concern on Ruth's face. "This is breaking my heart, too. If only she was older. Legally—"

"But she's not. And there's more." She slid the other letter over to Audrey. "From Nurse Lillian."

Audrey opened the letter and read the neatly printed lines.

> *Dear Ruth,*
>
> *Amelia came to me as you asked her to and I know more now about what has happened to her and what she is facing. Actually, I know too much now. You didn't realize the position that her coming to me would put me in, and I doubt that I would have been able to tell you not to.*
>
> *Ruth, I took a pledge when I became a nurse, and it is a pledge that I take seriously.*
>
> *Part of it states that "I will do all in my power to maintain and elevate the standard of my profession, and will hold in confidence all personal matters committed to my keeping, and all family affairs coming to my knowledge in the practice of my calling."*
>
> *It also states that "I will dedicate myself to devoted service to human welfare."*

I would not be writing you or sharing any of this with you if Amelia had not given me permission to talk with you. That permission and the trust I have in your concern for Amelia's safety is why you are receiving this.

She asked if she could stay with me and promised to clean house and do the laundry. And I had to tell her that it wasn't possible, that I could lose my job, or worse. But the knowledge that she will be in danger if she is sent home puts me in conflict, both personally and professionally.

I know that you have tried to build Amelia's confidence so that she can protect herself, but the threat from her father to institutionalize her is serious. I have strong reservations about what is often used as treatment. I have seen far more harm than good from using shock therapy and I believe it is used specifically on girls and women for the wrong reasons.

Audrey stood, leaving the letter on the table without reading the remainder. She didn't need to read more—couldn't. A spike of anxiety sent nervous energy twitching through her body, her thoughts unable to move past the words she hadn't expected. She paced a circle, hand to her forehead.

"What is it?" Ruth asked. "It's as bad as I thought, isn't it?"

The words shot fear through Audrey's heart. It was a danger so real that it made her heart pound its message in her ears. Her body tensed and heated and readied for flight as if the warning were for her. She took a deep breath and tried to clear her head and focus on the present. "We have to go get her," Audrey replied, and paced another tight circle. "The nurse is right," she said, finally making eye contact. "You have no idea."

"Tell me, then. Tell me what we should do. We can't just go get her."

It was contagious, the anxiety, the sense of urgency, passing from one to the other—refueled, re-sent. Audrey heard it in Ruth's voice, saw it in her eyes.

"Can the nurse help? Can you call her from your house?"

Ruth rose quickly. "Yes," she said. "I'll go right now."

Audrey followed her, under the corner of the sheet and to the door, where Ruth turned and wrapped her in a tight embrace. "Thank you," Ruth whispered against Audrey's ear, "for caring." She released her embrace but remained intimately close. "You don't even know Amelia."

"But I think I know you," Audrey replied, pushing against the urge to let the warmth pull her across the inches, to press into the full, red lips. She could let it all go—the worry, the guilt—for just a moment, just long enough to do what she had imagined so many times.

But it wasn't Audrey who crossed the inches. It happened so quickly, Ruth's lips touching hers for just a moment, and then gone. A moment only long enough to leave the promise of a long, sleepless night.

Chapter 21

The invitation to go to Nurse Lillian's house was God-sent. Now, more than any other time, it was important to focus on Amelia, to turn the fire of excitement and possibility that Ruth's kiss had ignited into fuel for a higher cause. A cause Audrey needed nearly as much as Amelia did.

They left immediately after the phone call and took the next train to Jackson. Determined and encouraged. The rumble of steel, powering past cornfields and pastures, sped them closer to a solution. Audrey felt it, almost a relief that they had a starting point. And she could tell that Ruth felt it, too, when she breached the narrow space between them and took Audrey's hand. It felt right, everything felt right.

The cab had barely stopped in front of the Barton house when the front screen door burst open and two excited girls bounded across the porch and down the steps to surround Ruth as she tried to exit the cab.

"Ruth, Ruth," they exclaimed, each trying to be heard over the other to welcome her. "I thought I'd never see you again" and "How long can you stay?" and "I have so much to tell you."

Two things were clear, Ruth was well-loved here and Nurse Lillian was blessed. Ruth glanced quickly over her shoulder to be sure Audrey was right behind her, and continued up to the house with a teenager attached to each arm.

Lillian met them on the porch with a smile that instantly took Audrey in. She reached between the chattering girls and hugged Ruth in a long, eyes-closed embrace. "It's so good to see you," she said as she released her. "Now, ignore all this chatter for a few moments and introduce us."

"Yes, of course," Ruth replied. Her cheeks were pink from excitement and she turned to pull Audrey closer. "This is my dear friend, Audrey, and this," she turned to the group of smiling women, "is Lillian and her daughters, Caroline and Katie—my family away from home."

Audrey took Lillian's outstretched hand. "I have heard such marvelous things about you. Thank you for inviting me today."

"Well, please come in. My husband will be home soon and you will meet the last piece of the Barton puzzle."

The chatter of questions began again before they could get settled in the living room.

"Did you read the book I gave you?" "Do you have a boyfriend?" "Have you read more Nancy Drew?" "I wish we could see you more often."

Ruth smiled and somehow managed the confusion. "Yes, I did." "No." "Four more Drews." "And so do I."

Before another barrage, Lillian stepped in. "Audrey, would you mind if you and I have a chat together and give the girls time to catch up with Ruth? I'm afraid the interruptions would make conversation useless otherwise."

"Not at all," Audrey replied. "I would love to have the chance to get to know you."

"Off you go, then," Lillian said to wide smiles of approval. "Get it out of your systems."

Audrey settled into one of two wingback chairs neatly placed on either side of an accent table.

"Ruth explained on the phone that she's told you how we know each other so we can talk comfortably," Lillian began.

"It isn't easy to trust someone with the hurting parts of yourself. I've never met anyone who has faced that part of themselves as directly as Ruth has."

"Over the years," Lillian said, "I've met so many girls, some shared their stories and some didn't. Some touched my heart more than others, and Ruth even more than the rest. And they all deserve better than the way they are treated—ostracized and blamed while the fathers escape judgment. Unless there has been some new development since I was in nursing school, it takes two to make a baby."

Audrey smiled, convinced now beyond doubt that every girl should have a mother like Lillian. "So I've heard," she replied.

"I took the extra hours at the Home to ease my heart. I do what I can to make this time in their lives better and let them know that someone still believes in their goodness."

"I see exactly why Ruth thinks so highly of you."

"She obviously trusts us both a great deal," Lillian replied. "We have to do our best not to let her down."

"Hey, Lil, I'm back," came a male voice from another part of the house. Robert Barton appeared around the corner of the kitchen with a smile and an introduction. "I picked up something for all you girls today," he said. "It's a surprise." He headed back to the kitchen, but stopped and poked his head around the corner. "It has lots of calories and it's chocolate."

Lillian gave him the big smile that he was waiting for. "At least a week's worth of brownie points," she said and added, "Will you go up and rescue Ruth from the girls? We're going to need some uninterrupted time. They can visit more at dinner."

∽ ∽ ∽

The circle tightened with Ruth on the couch and Audrey and Lillian's chairs pulled close. The tone of their conversation turned serious.

"I apologize," Ruth directed to Lillian. "I didn't realize what I was forcing you to do."

"No, Ruth, there is no need to apologize. What you did was the only thing you could do. We are all here to try to find a way to help Amelia."

Audrey spoke first. "I only know Amelia through what Ruth has told me, but I know all too well some of the danger that she is facing. And I want you to know that I will not allow her to be sent home. I'll do whatever it takes to make sure of that."

"I will, too," added Ruth.

The strength of their conviction seemed to surprise Lillian. She hesitated a moment before saying, "I will do everything I can to help Amelia—legally. But anything that crosses that line I can't be involved in. As much as I might be tempted to listen to my heart, I have to be careful. I need to be here for my family, for my patients, and for my girls at the Home. I just can't do anything that will jeopardize that, but I will do everything else that I can."

"So let's work backward from the premise that she is not going home," Audrey began. "We know that she can't stay with you, Lillian. Can she stay with either of us?"

"Robert's brother is an attorney, so he was the first person I talked to. Since she is not of age, if you transport her you can be charged with kidnapping. If she gets there on her own, you could be guilty of harboring a runaway." Lillian looked directly at Ruth. "And because of how close you were with her at the Home, they will look at your place first."

"Then I don't see any way around *someone* doing something illegal," Ruth said.

"Or *somebodies*," added Audrey. "Do you think we could make our own underground railroad, like the slaves used?"

"There is something else we have to consider," Lillian said. "A runaway girl, and that's what our Amelia will be, is even more likely to be institutionalized if she gets caught." Her expression heightened in directness and seated the message. The stakes had just gone up. The words seared through Audrey's senses.

Ruth asked the obvious question. "How can we find people who will care as much as we do—who will be willing to take those kinds of chances for someone they don't know?"

"Someone who has experienced something like what Amelia is facing," Audrey offered. "Wouldn't they want to help prevent her from going through the same thing?"

"I may know someone," Lillian offered.

"And maybe that person will know someone else," Ruth added. "And then that person may know someone."

"We won't have much time to put things in place," Lillian said. "I see Amelia Monday and I'll have a little better idea how close she is to delivering. We're going to have to stay in phone contact every day."

"Here's the number where I'm staying." Ruth pulled a pencil and small pad of paper from her purse, wrote the number, and handed it to Lillian. "I'll call you tonight with the number at the restaurant, if that's all right."

"Yes." Lillian looked first at Ruth and then Audrey. "We're going to do this, then?"

"*Even*," Audrey said, "if I have to kidnap her right out of that hospital bed."

కళ కళ కళ

Audrey knew it was coming, the inevitable question. She had laid the path to it carefully, purposefully. It let Ruth walk along with her, until now, until it was the right time to answer.

They talked about Lillian and her commitment, and Amelia and the possibility of their plan. But Ruth had waited to ask until they sat in the darkness of the back seat of the cab.

Blessed by a non-talkative driver listening to the news on the radio, Ruth asked softly, "Will you tell me why you are so passionate about helping Amelia, aside from the dangers that we both know she is facing?"

Being prepared to answer a question was one thing, a fairly well-controlled thing. What Audrey couldn't prepare for was answering it while her body was betraying her. The space was too close, too dark. There were no bright restaurant lights or busy conversations to diffuse the flush of her skin or the pounding of her heart. And no brief whiffs of Ruth's perfume or brushes against her arm with relief only seconds away. Tonight there was no escaping the familiar scent overcoming the oddness of the taxi's space, or the heat radiating through the fabric of her skirt where Ruth's thigh pressed against it.

Audrey tried to concentrate on the words. "I let someone down," she began, "someone I loved—love very much." A slow stream of light from approaching headlights temporarily exposed the look she'd seen from only one other, the same look she had promised to never encourage again, the look she longed for. "I didn't protect her. I didn't know how." Ruth's hand slipped underneath hers and laced their fingers together. "I don't know if she is capable of forgiving me. And

129

until you came to me about Amelia, I thought that my only redemption was to never put another in that kind of danger."

"Danger because she loved you?"

Audrey turned her head to the window. It wasn't this answer that made her hesitate, it was the one that was surely to follow. "Yes," she returned softly.

"Do you still believe that?"

"The danger hasn't changed."

"And it's happening again," Ruth said, and touched her fingers beneath Audrey's chin to turn her head back. "Someone's loving you."

The words spoken so softly and holding such power, stopped her breath. Audrey forced herself to take the next breath, dared to stay with the look Ruth was sending through the darkness, promising what seemed impossible.

"*I'm* loving you," Ruth whispered as close to Audrey's lips as she dared. "If you feel the same thing . . . I need you to tell me."

"From the moment you said, 'I don't know where you are from, sir.' That . . . confidence," she replied, gently squeezing Ruth's hand, "the hold of your head and the set of your shoulders. I knew that you would challenge every fear that I have."

"Can you see my smile?"

"Yes," she said, touching fingertips to the smooth, warm skin of Ruth's cheeks.

"I will challenge every one of them, whatever they are, for as long as it takes for you to be free of them."

"Then you need to know what it is that I fear. Will you come with me tomorrow so that I can show you?"

"When do we leave?"

Chapter 22

The early morning air was cool and smelled of warm metal. The two women boarded the train and took their seats. There was an odd feeling of excitement, or maybe it was anticipation, but something niggled at Ruth's thoughts. She had hungered to know more about this woman since she first saw her sitting alone, strangely content, in the restaurant. Throughout the months since then she had gathered everything she could about who Audrey Draper was—what made her smile, what made her bristle, what made her proud. Audrey liked casseroles and pork chops and cherry pie and ice cream. Good hot food at the end of a long shift made her smile even when no one was watching. She steeled her jaw at insinuations that she was "less than." She was proud of her part in the war effort and, it seemed, she was proud of Ruth Evans. It had been a long time, Ruth thought, since anyone had been proud of her.

What she did not know was what Audrey feared, specifically, personally. Not the usual fears of a woman on her own, not the expected fears of a woman loving another woman, but *her* fears. Those so deep, and so well-protected that they could cause Audrey to give up any chance to love again. Today, though, Ruth knew that she was going to find out.

"Her name is Velma," Audrey said, turning to look at Ruth. "I want you to know her."

Ruth waited attentively as Audrey's eyes refocused vaguely at the landscape passing them by. "The first time I saw her she was wading in the fountain in the park. She didn't seem to care at all that her skirt was wet to her knees. She talked me into wading with her. I'd never felt so free. We laughed and splashed each other and drew disapproving looks, and I decided right then that I wanted her to be a part of every day. And she was. I thought she was beautiful, her hair always down, loose and free, and a smile so easy and bright. She dreamed and wondered and asked, why not? We shared everything with each other, the simplest things that made us happy, our loftiest dreams, our love. We stole time—moments, hours—and lied to everyone except each other. We laughed and sang and loved and dreamed, and never spoke of what might happen if we were found out. We were happy and in love. No one could take that joy from us because we were invincible."

She was talking about a lost love, a love she still held. Ruth watched her as she looked past the window, past the moving landscape, past her, and wondered how much pain this journey was bringing. How hard was it to lose a pureness that she was sure she'd never have again?

The impulse to pull Audrey into her arms and hold her through the pain, to tell her that Ruth would be there with her through the journey was so strong, so hard to override. She wondered if Velma would have asked, *why not?* Would the right thing to do have won? Would hers have been the answer that ignored the risks and allowed Ruth to pull Audrey close and hold her?

Ruth slipped her hand under Audrey's, her compromise. Audrey turned from the window and the train slowed into the station.

"Thank you," Audrey said, "for listening."

"You never have to thank me for that."

People began leaving their seats and making their way down the aisle. "I hope you will understand why I am doing this," Audrey said as they rose.

"I think I already do."

∽ ∽ ∽

Audrey hadn't said a word during the cab ride. She sat as if she would exit at any moment and fidgeted with the clasp on the slender brown purse on her lap. The cab dropped them at the front walk, a long, deliberate distance leading to the most intimidating building Ruth had ever seen. The immense three-story brick building warned of a familiar isolation and judgment that Ruth knew too well. She fought apprehension, matched Audrey's pace, and followed her lead.

After the long silence in the cab, it was unexpected when partway down the walk Audrey asked, "Do you attend church?"

The question seemed an odd one. "Obligatory attendance when I lived at home. My parents are Catholic, it was expected. I'm relishing the time I have now to figure out what I am."

"I come here every Sunday that I can. I come here to try to find redemption, even though I know that I never will. That kind of thinking makes it sound like I should be locked up here, too, doesn't it?"

Ruth looked over, unsure of what to say, but Audrey continued looking straight ahead and didn't seem to need a response.

"The first time I walked this walk, so determined, so set on my mission, it was to ask for forgiveness." She hesitated for a moment, and then added, "and to take Velma away from this place." They stopped before going through the large wooden door. "And the first time through these doors was when I realized how dangerous naivety is."

There was only the necessary interaction from detached hospital personnel as the women signed in at the visitor's desk and were led down the corridor to the day room. Unlike the common room at the Crittenton Home, filled with overstuffed seating and conversation, the day room was stiff and sterile and strangely quiet. Women sat in chairs lining the walls and beside large unadorned windows. Some mumbled incoherently or talked to no one in particular. Others rocked from side to side in straight-back chairs or stared blankly ahead. An isolation beyond what she had experienced at the Home—beyond her comprehension.

Audrey found Velma at a window at the far end of the room. She made no attempt to turn her stare from the window as Audrey knelt beside her chair.

"Velma," she said, placing her hand over Velma's, folded neatly in her lap, "it's Audrey. I've brought someone to meet you." She cupped her hand under Velma's chin and gently brought her head around to face her. There was no expression, no recognition in Velma's eyes.

Beautiful blue eyes with the glassiness of a doll's. Audrey stroked Velma's cheek and tried again. "It's me, Velma. It's Audrey."

A soft crease developed between Velma's brows. Her voice sounded tired. "Is it time for dinner?"

"No, sweetie," Audrey replied, then cupped Velma's chin again when she started to turn back toward the window. "I've come to visit with you, and I brought someone to meet you." Audrey reached for Ruth's hand and pulled her to kneel beside her. "This is Ruth, Velma, she's a friend. I wanted her to meet you."

The pretty eyes looked close at Audrey's face as if trying to recall, the struggle pushing into a deep frown. They moved to Ruth's face and the frown lines eased. The struggle ended and the glassiness returned.

"Her name is Ruth, Velma. I've told her about how we met and our favorite place. Do you remember the fountain?" Velma turned past Audrey and fixed her stare once more out the window. But Audrey persisted, moving to sit against the windowsill in front of Velma. She reached her hand out to Ruth to join her. "Remember how cool the water felt, how we stood under the water flowing from the mouth of the big fish in the center?" A start of a frown, only a twitch this time. Audrey surveyed the face that used to show such joy, and waited.

Ruth watched Audrey carefully begin removing the bobby pins holding Velma's dark hair in tight rolls atop her head. The care, the expression on Audrey's face brought a painful tightness to Ruth's throat. She took a deep breath trying to relieve it as Audrey loosened the unpinned hair and let it fall freely to Velma's shoulders.

"Your mother was here, I know," Audrey said, letting her fingers loosen the heavy tresses. "She always hated your hair down."

Velma tilted her head and ran her hands through her hair. A break from her world, however slight, but enough to brighten Audrey's face. "That feels better, doesn't it?" she said. "I know how you love it loose and free."

The tinge of hopefulness Ruth saw in Audrey's face, heard in her voice, brought the tightness back to her throat. How can she put herself through this? How many times? How can love be so deep, and so painful? So real. Not a past or a story left to the imagination, but flesh-and-blood real.

Audrey took Velma's hands in her own and asked, "What shall we talk about today? What would make you smile? Oh, I know," she said, touching Velma's face to get her to look up. "I heard one of your favorite Cole Porter songs on the radio the other night. Do you remember when you did *Red, Hot and Blue* with the Civic Theater? You sang 'It's De-lovely,' and you sang it to me in the park. You sing so beautifully."

There was still no response from Velma, no recognition, only the blank stare. Audrey began humming the song softly, enough of it that Ruth recognized it. She watched her, trying so hard, caring so much, and realized that the love she felt for Audrey was reaching a depth she hadn't expected. But was it possible for it to ever match the love she was witnessing?

"The night is young, the skies are clear," Audrey sang the words now, bending forward, challenging the pretty, empty eyes. She sang the next line, and then something happened. The stare never changed, but when Audrey began the chorus, "It's delightful," Velma's light, whispery tone joined, "it's delicious, it's de-lovely."

Audrey continued singing and Velma sang with her the second verse and the chorus again, and the third. Tears began streaming down Audrey's cheeks but she kept singing, holding Velma's hands and leaning close.

Ruth smiled, despite the tightness in her throat giving way to her own tears. It was more emotion than she was ready for—raw and honest and beyond what she had expected. She stepped to the window, allowed the tears as she stared at the blurry landscape. Not watching, though, did not stop the tears. The vision was unshakably vivid—the glimmer behind Audrey's tears, was it hope? And if it was, wasn't it tragic in itself? She couldn't find an answer. Maybe there wasn't one, not one that could explain what she was seeing, what she was feeling. All she could do was let emotion overrun its bounds, and let the tears try to soothe the pain she couldn't identify. If *this* was so difficult, how could she ever soothe Audrey's pain?

Audrey had begun the song again from the beginning, and kept singing until Velma's voice dropped off. She tried the chorus once again, but Velma had stopped singing.

Ruth quickly wiped the tears from her cheeks, and turned from the window to find Audrey with her forehead pressed against Velma's. Agitation nearby, a patient circling too close to another patient's chair, brought a staff member over to control the situation. She directed the patient to the center of the room, and walked back over to announce "Visiting hours are over. You will have to leave now."

Audrey never looked up. She pressed her lips to the side of Velma's head and whispered something in her ear. Velma made no response, there was no acknowledgment in the eyes staring straight ahead. Audrey wiped her cheeks with her hands as she straightened, then smoothed her hand over the free, dark tresses before she left.

The pace Audrey set was quick and determined. Ruth matched her steps, a silent retreat through the long hallway and down the walk from the building to the street.

"Shouldn't we have called for a cab?" Ruth asked as Audrey turned down the sidewalk between a tall iron fence and the street.

"I need to walk, Ruth," she said without breaking stride. "I'm sorry."

"No, don't be sorry. We'll walk as long as you want."

They walked for miles with no small talk, no conversation at all. If this was how Audrey needed to work through the pain, Ruth would respect it, no matter how long it took or how many miles they walked. The hardest part was watching the woman that she was growing to love more each day struggle alone, and not know how to help her.

Audrey was nearly as unresponsive as Velma when they finally traveled home, mustering only an occasional "I'm okay" to Ruth's concerns. It wasn't convincing. How could it be? Ruth had decided before they got off the train that she wasn't leaving her alone tonight.

They stood at Audrey's door and she repeated her plea, "I just need to be alone."

"Not tonight," Ruth replied. "Not after today. You don't have to talk about it, that's fine. Just let me talk." Audrey's expression looked more like relief than resignation. Convinced that this was where she needed to be tonight, Ruth took Audrey's hand to have her sit on the edge of the bed with her. But Audrey wasn't ready to talk or to sit. She slipped her hand from Ruth's, put her purse on the table, and walked to the small window at the back of the room.

"I understand," Ruth began, "why you wanted me to go with you today. I couldn't know you without seeing Velma, without seeing you with her. I saw how deeply you love. I saw at least a little of how hard losing what you had with her has been on you. And there was something else I saw. I'm not sure what it was. When Velma started singing I saw it in your eyes . . . Was it hope, Audrey?"

Audrey tilted her head back and spoke toward the ceiling. "No," she said, and turned to face Ruth. "Not hope. You saw what I saw, the only part of Velma I have left." She stepped quickly past Ruth, across the room, an abrupt turn and then back again. Her voice rose in anger, her hand sliced the air as she spoke. "They took away hope, they took her life just as if they had put a gun to her head and pulled the trigger." Her eyes held a fierceness Ruth had not seen. "They sent electric current through her to erase what was wrong with her brain." She stepped closer. "What was *wrong*—because she didn't follow the rules, because she loved *me*." Tears streamed down Audrey's face. The fierceness in her eyes had morphed into something else. "They erased it all," her voice began to waiver, "everything that was good, they took it all." Then in a final burst of anger, she shouted, "What right did they have? What *right?*" She stood there in the middle of the room, quivering and spent, her eyes pleading for an answer.

Ruth went to her quickly, wrapped her arms tightly around her, and felt Audrey's body slacken. She had given up, released the anger that had bound her all this time, and finally let it go.

"Come here," Ruth said, pulling a willing Audrey onto the bed with her. She wrapped herself around Audrey and cradled her as she cried. There was nothing to say, not yet. The heart of it had been said. What was important now was for her to feel someone else's arms around her. She didn't need to be strong now, Ruth would be that strength for her. This was her time to cry as hard and as long as she needed for the cleansing. It was Audrey's time. Ruth's would come soon enough.

How long she held Audrey like that, stroking her head, kissing her forehead, Ruth couldn't say. It didn't matter, she was there when Audrey needed her. She wanted to promise that she would always be.

The last of the sunlight shining through the window had long since turned to a hazy blue-gray, and now the room was quickly darkening. Audrey rested calmly, her face snugged into the warm vee of Ruth's neck. She stirred enough to slide her arm around Ruth's back and to whisper, "I can't let her go."

"I know," Ruth replied softly. "It's okay."

"I love you, Ruth. But the Velma that she used to be tears at my heart."

"If she didn't, if you *had* just let her go, I don't think I would love you like I do."

Audrey leaned away to look into Ruth's eyes. "You aren't afraid of this love, are you?"

"And that worries you, doesn't it?"

"Velma wasn't afraid either, she was just honestly who she was, and it destroyed her."

Ruth ventured the next question. "Why her and not you?"

"Because I'm a liar," Audrey said as she sat up. "I will lie and deny, and compromise who I am to survive. Not traits to be applauded, or to be proud of. Is that a woman you can love?"

Ruth sat up next to her. "I've lied, Audrey. Maybe not as successfully as you, but I've lied and compromised. Unlike you, though, I didn't just lie to others. I lied to myself. What I was doing was for everyone else. The only one surviving was who they thought I was, while the real me was dying. I had to learn what you somehow have known all along—that whatever we have to do, we do to protect who we are."

Ruth stood and straightened her skirt. Audrey remained on the edge of the bed, her focus on the floor. Ruth touched the top of her head and said, "It's been a hard day, and I *do* understand your fears. I understand a lot of things, Audrey, so there's no need to test me anymore." She turned and started toward the door. She had been there with her through the anger and the sadness, and now she was sure that Audrey needed to be alone. Nothing about either of their lives was simple, and nothing was going to be resolved tonight.

Audrey's voice behind her was sharp, raised above conversation level. "I'm not testing you. It's me I'm testing, Ruth. I'm testing *me*."

Ruth turned to see Audrey standing in the middle of the room, her fist clenched tightly against her chest. "What inside of me," she continued, "in this heart, in this conflicted head of mine, can I believe? What do I trust? The truth is, I don't know. Maybe the love that I feel is so wrong that it poisons anyone who touches it. Will I poison you, too? Destroy you as I have Velma?"

"Oh, no," Ruth said, returning to pull Audrey into an embrace. "No, honey, no." She clasped the back of Audrey's head and held it firmly against her own. "It's me here, just me. No one else. No parents, no husband or boyfriend, no one. No one knows me except you." She pressed her lips to Audrey's neck, kissed it again and again. "There's no one in my life but you," she whispered. "No love but yours. There's no one to take it away."

"How can you be sure?"

Ruth loosened the firmness of her hold and lifted her head to look into Audrey's eyes. "Because I know me now," she said softly. "The only doubts are yours. The only fears are yours." She traced her thumb over the high cheekbone, felt the warm flush from Audrey's face against her palm. "Believe me," she whispered, as her eyes traveled to the natural pale pink of Audrey's lips. "Believe this." She kissed Audrey, full and firm, and sent a flood of heat through their bodies that neither of them could deny. They both knew the course of it— the heat deep and low, spikes of excitement defining a need that would consume them. But it wouldn't go there yet, not tonight.

Ruth lifted her lips, left with one last light kiss, and backed toward the door. "Dream of me tonight," she said, "as I will you."

Chapter 23

Dear Amelia,

I have wings now, as sleek and shiny and strong as the ones that take the Liberator into battle. I can soar now—as high as my hopes and as far as my imagination.

I'm free, Amelia. I'm free to explore and imagine and accomplish, and even to fail. Failure doesn't scare me, that's how I am going to know what I want for my life. Nor does wondering and thinking about the possibilities for my life scare me. It's exciting to see what's possible, for me and for other women, and for you.

Women have accomplished such wonderful things. And why not? We are smart and resourceful, we're strong of will and determined. We are all of that, Amelia. I am and you are, too.

Don't be afraid to test your wings. Let them hold you up and keep you safe. Trust us for a plan and trust your wings to make it happen.

Her letters, until now, had been Ruth's only answer to the worry that had consumed her for months. And until this one, sending them off in the mail had offered at least a temporary relief. She'd done all she could do, as well as she could do it. But, this time, instead of relief she felt the fear of time running out without a plan in place. She had made a promise that she might not be able to keep.

And if she failed her promise, failed Amelia, how could she ever read another of her letters? How could she know the truth in the words and go on, untouched? There was no way to unknow what she knew, or stop the images that her knowledge allowed. There had been no frightening images before Audrey, before Velma—only a sketchy and fleeting image of Amelia's uncle. She had needed a picture of him in her mind in order to create a place for her disgust, and to separate it from her empathy. It had been enough at the time. Then, she had listened and empathized. Had advised and made it a daily practice to bolster Amelia's self-confidence. All the while she was sure that she understood.

But she didn't understand, not really. She had never herself felt the clutch of fear that governed Amelia's world, or the repulsion that grew out of her vulnerability. Ruth had never had to endure repeated violations to her body and her spirit, or live with the knowledge that she had no power to stop it. What she saw and what she understood, at least in its simplest form, were the consequences. Amelia's consequences, and now Velma's.

Beyond that, she was only beginning to recognize her own consequences. Without Audrey, without Velma, she wondered how much longer it might have taken. Would she have dared to consider the role of savior, dared to take on such a serious responsibility? What made her think that she was smart enough, resourceful enough, brave enough?

How long she'd been staring out her bedroom window she couldn't say. But for at least that long she had been looking at an important part of a plan, one that just might work. It had been sitting in Mrs. Welly's driveway all along.

Ruth rushed downstairs and into the front room, startling her landlady from her reading. "Oh, Ruth! What is it? What's wrong?"

"No, no, nothing's wrong, Mrs. Welly. In fact, it's possibly just the opposite." Ruth dropped into the chair, her excitement barely contained. "The car in the driveway," she began, "do you ever use it?"

"Oh, Lord, no. I wouldn't even know how to start it," she replied. "Not sure it would start even if I knew how. It's been sittin' there as long as my husband's been gone."

"Have you ever thought about selling it?"

"Never got around to it. I thought maybe my son-in-law might want it, but he has a newer model and doesn't need it."

"Can I buy it from you?"

"For you? You want to buy it for yourself?"

"Yes."

Mrs. Welly seemed to be trying to grasp a reason for the request. "Do you know how to drive a car?"

"No," Ruth said, "not yet."

"Why on earth would you even want to learn?"

"There's something important I need to do, Mrs. Welly."

"Well, then, if that car's going to help you, it's yours."

👁 👁 👁

Her excitement couldn't wait until tomorrow. Ruth took the next bus to Audrey's and anxiously waited on her front step to tell her the good news. It wouldn't matter how long she had to wait, the plan was too important. And for the first time it felt like a real plan was close—not just a hope or an *if only*, but a real course of action was coming together. Her own fear had already bowed its head. Now to assuage Audrey's.

She used the hour or so of waiting to think about what needed to come next. The pieces seemed so feasible—get the car running, learn to drive it, prepare Amelia—but the one big *if*, the last important piece, was up to Lillian.

The sun began its descent late in the evening this time of year, and Ruth could see Audrey walking down from the bus stop. Even these last few minutes were too long to wait. Ruth stood, lifted her skirt above her knees, and ran to meet her.

If not for the wide smile, a woman running at her down the middle of the street might have given Audrey serious concern. Ruth let the smile carry the message until she was two doors away. "Great news," she called out. "I've got great news." She closed the distance and, breathing hard, wrapped Audrey in an excited hug.

"Tell me," Audrey said as Ruth released her. "What?"

"I have a car. I mean, I will have a car. It might not start, so we have to find a battery. Oh, and I'll have to learn to drive it."

"Whoa, slow down." Audrey said. "Come on, let's get in and sit down. I'm so tired."

By the time they plopped onto the kitchen chairs, Audrey, too, was bristling with excitement. "Wait, Ruth. You don't have to worry about learning to drive. I can drive it. And I can teach you."

"Oh, Audrey, it *is* happening. Our plan is coming together. I've been so worried." She stopped for a moment to appreciate Audrey's smile. She hadn't seen it nearly enough lately. Then she asked, "How did you learn to drive?"

"Velma," she replied. "My wonderful, daringly unconventional Velma." The smile was still there but had softened with reflection. "She watched her father every day, riding to work with him. She remembered every move he made. Then while he was working she would take the keys from his jacket pocket and practice driving the car all around the parking lot."

"Oh, a firecracker to be sure."

Audrey nodded before her smile dissolved. "She was."

"Tell me how she taught you to drive." Her tactic was obvious but effective.

"She stole her father's car right out of the parking lot, picked me up, and we spent the whole afternoon driving in the country. She was so good, like she had been driving for years. It was a beautiful sight— the window down, her hair blowing around her face as she sang to me, singing to the world . . . I didn't think it would be so easy—driving. But it was. And not only in the country. I drove right through town as if I were going to work or shopping or visiting friends. I've never felt anything quite like it. Driving that car was liberating, Ruth. When I was behind the wheel I was in control. I knew I could go anywhere I wanted, anytime I wanted. The world felt different, like I had my hands on its direction. I could make it fly by me, tempt me with stopping here or stopping there. And I would decide. I could make it be still for as long as I wanted—long enough for baby goats, bouncing and baying in a famer's field, to make me laugh, or for a river, tumbling over rocks under a bridge to make me wonder where it went."

As she watched her, Ruth realized that Audrey wasn't merely telling a story, she was igniting possibility. What Ruth heard was a description of the world as she, too, wanted to experience it. A world with possibilities she hadn't even imagined, possibilities she wanted to experience with Audrey.

"We took the car a lot," Audrey continued. "We drove and sang and explored, and we knew we would find a way to have our own car. It was part of our future."

"Did she ever get caught?"

"Not by her father. Someone he worked with came out to get something out of his car just after Velma had parked it. But the timing was as lucky as it gets. She had just filled a bucket with water and begun washing the dust from it to hide that we'd been driving in the country. He thought that she had to be the perfect daughter to be washing her father's car while he was working. She laughed when she told me about it, and said it was the only time she would ever be considered the perfect daughter." Audrey hesitated and answered with a frown. "She was right."

It felt as if a brisk spring breeze had been sucked into a vacuum. The air was suffocatingly still.

"I'm going to go sit in our car tonight," Ruth began, "and imagine I'm driving and feeling everything you described."

The corners of Audrey's mouth lifted gently. "I promise I'll give you the real thing. I'll see if Jack can help us find a battery. And since I'm a government worker, I'll see if I can get the gas voucher."

Ruth reached across the table and took Audrey's hands. "We're really going to do this, aren't we?"

Audrey squeezed Ruth's hands tightly. "If I have to drive her into Canada myself."

"And if I have to quit my job and move to Canada to take care of her," Ruth added.

"No one is going to do to Amelia what they did to Velma, I promise you that."

Her heart pounded, her eyes stayed with Audrey's and claimed their promise. "I love you, Audrey Draper."

Audrey stood and pulled Ruth into an embrace.

The arms holding her told Ruth what words could not. They held her, firm and sure, finally offering promise instead of doubt. Ruth pressed tightly into the promise, accepted it for whatever it meant. The beat of her heart jumped free, quickened its rhythm against Audrey's breast. Her body shared the heat between them, and the smooth flush of skin as Audrey pressed her face against Ruth's. Exactly where she wanted to be, exactly what she needed.

Audrey whispered the words. "Please don't let this be the worst thing to happen to you."

Ruth leaned back to see the concern in Audrey's eyes, and offered softly, "I can lie with the best of them if need be." She slid the palm of her hand gently over Audrey's cheek. "And the only person I promise not to lie to is you." It was all she had, all that she could promise. And it was enough.

Audrey said so without words. She said it in her kiss and Ruth believed it, welcomed it. This was no mistake. It was love—in all its splendor and its risks—warm and sweet and taking away her breath.

The kiss lingered and wandered, and was answered with another. Tender touches at first, exploring and deepening. Whispers found space. "Stay with me."

"Yes."

This was their time, their space, safe and protected. Between kisses they found buttons and zippers and hooks, and slid together between the coolness of the sheets. Ruth's lips touched the smooth flesh of Audrey's neck, trailed fervent kisses down the curve to its base, and felt Audrey's body respond. Long, lean legs entwined with her own, arms wrapped her tightly, and Audrey returned kisses to Ruth's face and neck.

Ruth closed her eyes and breathed in the sweet lilac scent of the silky dark hair falling over her cheek. It felt so right—the feel of Audrey's body against her own, the flush of her skin, the quickening of her heart. Nothing could be more right—this love, this woman—reaching for her, wanting her.

Audrey slid her fingers into Ruth's hair, grasped the side of Ruth's head, and covered her mouth with a kiss that pressed her back into the pillow. There was no more need for thought or worry or anything, only accepting—the kisses now growing in urgency, the desire searing through her, the love. Audrey's love. Yes, she accepted it all, fully and wholly.

She needed nothing more, wanted nothing more. Ruth let go of everything, gave it up to the sensations racing through her body, to the need to go wherever Audrey took her. Ruth had no control, welcoming the free fall as Audrey's hips moved against her and Audrey's hands defined and caressed her body. She wanted Audrey's lips everywhere, her tongue circling her breasts, teasing her neck, probing their kisses, bringing her to the place where sensations race ahead on their own. Racing to that glorious place she knew, this time with whispers she had longed for.

"I love you," Audrey breathed, low against her neck. "Do you know?"

"Yes, oh yes." Ruth whispered in return. "I know, my love, I know." She wanted to say more, to tell her how much she trusted those words, how much she believed in her heart, but words would wait. It was her body speaking now, gathering the whispers, the caresses, the heat into a need sounding through soft moans and gasps of desire—hers, Audrey's, *theirs* together. No separation, no delineation, only a melting that fused them, flesh to flesh. Only the want was clear, driving them harder, faster, until she couldn't stop, wouldn't stop her body from shouting in joy and release. She was in that beautiful place at last, sensations rippling in decreasing waves, passion settling into gentle kisses over the moist, flushed skin of Audrey's face and neck.

Audrey returned kisses to Ruth's neck and nestled her face against her shoulder. She wrapped her arms and legs around Ruth in a snug embrace and said softly, "My sweet love, you've filled my heart."

She felt the beating of Audrey's heart against her breast. "It's where I always want to be," Ruth whispered. "Always."

Chapter 24

Maybe it was her internal clock, or maybe it was a need to be conscious of every moment that Ruth was in her arms, but Audrey was wide awake long before necessary.

The early morning stillness allowed her mind to move freely, without interruption, over the string of events that had brought Ruth into her heart. Unpredictable. Unimaginable. Even now, with Ruth snuggled against her chest, Audrey wondered at how it happened. How circumstances in each of their lives had brought them here, to each other. Things that had threatened to destroy their chances at happiness had instead made happiness possible. And neither of them would have predicted it.

Her own healing was next to miraculous—guilt slowly giving way to forgiveness and understanding, hate and fear losing out to resolve and a newfound courage. The ache in her heart now had a balm to soothe it.

All this was part of her realization. But she wondered, as Ruth stirred awake, about Ruth's healing. She never spoke of her own struggle. Yet it had to be there, tucked deep, overridden at least outwardly by concern for Amelia and her concern for a new love.

"Don't wake me," Ruth whispered, her eyes still closed, "if this isn't real."

Audrey shifted from the position she'd held to keep from waking Ruth. "Then I'll kiss you awake," she said, pressing her lips to Ruth's forehead.

"What has you awake so early?" Ruth asked.

"Thinking about you."

"Oh?" Ruth smiled and laid back against the pillow. "What is it you're thinking?"

"How much I love you." As her eyes adjusted to the darkness she met Ruth's gaze. "And how selfless you are. It makes me worry about you."

"No, you mustn't worry about me. Honey, don't. I'm fine."

Audrey turned onto her side. "Not about this," she said. "Not about us loving each other. I worry that you care so much about Amelia and about me that you're not getting what *you* need."

"What I need is to know that Amelia will be okay. And I need your love."

"But you've said so little about what you've gone through. I can't imagine how I would feel in your place. Is there the same kind of guilt and sadness?"

There were a few seconds of hesitation before Ruth answered. "I'm okay. I've dealt with it. Really," she said, stroking the side of Audrey's face. "There's nothing to worry about."

"Would you trust me with it if there was?"

"Yes," Ruth replied, "of course I would."

"Because I'm here. You don't have to hurt alone. I'll always listen. You can tell me anything—and I'll help any way I can. I want you to know that."

Ruth slipped her arm across the smooth skin of Audrey's back and pulled her into an embrace. "If there is one thing I know for sure about you, it's that. Velma taught me all I need to know. She showed me your heart."

Chapter 25

There had been days, pink with romance and giddy with love, memorable for their place in Audrey's life. And there had been steel-cold days and dark, desperate nights that challenged her hope for anything else.

The structure of those days had changed very little. She worked the same hours, ate dinner at The Bomber, and spent her usual evenings with Nona. All the same stresses, the same responsibilities and exhaustion still rolled along during the course of each day, but without their usual notice. Now, shining above it all, every day, were visions of Ruth—tactile, sensual, an inextinguishable brightness.

Unlike the past months of hedging and worrying, the days and nights of arguing back desire and possibility, the first thing in Audrey's thoughts was how soon she would see Ruth. She was in love, and happy—like before, with Velma. This time, though, she was in love and well aware of the risks.

Everything lately had an air of excitement about it, and today was no exception. Jack had found a battery and as fast as they could get out of the plant, they were on their way to Ruth's.

Jack chattered the whole way across town, wondering about the car and asking questions that Audrey couldn't answer. By the time they arrived at Ruth's driveway, Audrey had heard the story of Jack's first car in detail and realized that his love of cars came in a tight number three behind his love of his wife and new baby.

"1935 model 48," he said before he even got out of the car. He jumped out and continued as he circled Ruth's new acquisition. "Fordor Humpback."

Ruth burst from the side door of the house. "What do you think, Jack?"

"Oh, it's a beauty," he said. "Yes, it is."

"She's been sittin' for a bit," Ruth replied. "But I'll bet she is a beauty under that layer of dust."

"We'll give her a proper wash after we get her started," Audrey offered, sending a smile in Ruth's direction.

"Yep, we'll get her started," Jack said. He pulled the battery and a wrench from the trunk of his car and met the two women at the top of the driveway. "Uh, huh," he said after lifting the hood, "refreshed 221 CID V8. She's gonna hum."

Audrey hovered over the fender and watched him take out the old battery and replace it. If she was going to drive a car she ought to know how it worked.

It took a can of fresh gas and three tries and Jack had the car humming just as he had promised. "Jump in," he said. "I'll move my car, and then we'll take this beauty for a spin and clean out her system."

Through the neighborhood, and out for a short distance on the highway in order to get it just over the speed limit at forty miles an hour, and Jack was pleased. Audrey was grateful, for his help and his friendship, and for his acceptance. He never questioned why, about anything.

෨ ෨ ෨

"You were right," exclaimed Ruth, her hands firmly on the steering wheel. "We're really free, aren't we?" The car rolled at a leisurely pace down the dirt road just outside of town, and Ruth checked her mirrors religiously, exactly as Audrey had instructed. No cars ahead of them and none behind, just as it had been for miles, but practice made good habits.

"Turn into this farmer's drive coming up," Audrey directed. "Go a little further this time and then back up to the road and turn around. We'd better head back home before dark. We'll get you used to driving at night another time."

Backing up was getting somewhat easier. She was learning to trust her mirrors and not stick her head out the window. But coordinating releasing the clutch and giving it the right amount of gas still needed work. The car bucked and lunged in defiance. Ruth gritted her teeth and willed herself to get it right.

The car smoothed out and Ruth asked, "Should I have this by now? How many times have you had me stop and start and go through the gears? I want to be as good a driver as you are."

"You will be," Audrey replied. "Maybe even better. Anyone who can balance a tray of dinners above her shoulder, wind her way between tables, and not hit a customer or spill a drop can do anything she sets her mind to."

"I sure hope you're right because I want to do this every day for the rest of my life. I don't know how to describe how this makes me feel."

Audrey answered Ruth's quick, wide-eyed turn of her head with a huge smile. "Better than fully loaded ice cream?"

"Oh, yes, even that. This is something that I've never felt before." She chanced another quick glance to see Audrey waiting. But the words to describe it weren't there. How could she describe the feel of the engine vibrating from the steering wheel through her hands and arms? Or the realization that she was controlling something so large, a machine capable of taking her wherever she decided? Decisions and a power that were all hers.

"Is it wrong," Ruth asked, "that I feel powerful right now?"

Audrey slid closer and pressed her lips to Ruth's cheek. "No," she said. "And I think this is only the beginning." Ruth's eyes remained on the road, but Audrey could tell that she was smiling. "You go right ahead and feel powerful."

Ruth loosened and re-gripped the polished wood of the steering wheel and let her smile linger a little longer. This was a feeling she would never let go. "Yes, this is only the beginning." She pulled the car to a stop at the side of the road. "But I would rather you take us the rest of the way home through town. I don't want to risk any damage my first time out."

⤜ ⤜ ⤜

153

Audrey delivered them safely to Mrs. Welly's driveway, turned off the engine, and handed the key to Ruth. "Another lesson tomorrow?"

"Yes, yes," Ruth replied. "I can't wait." She took Audrey's hand and squeezed it tightly. "That powerful girl that was behind the wheel would kiss you with authority, but she's taking her leave for this more reasonable head." She placed her hand gently to the side of Audrey's face. "So I'll just say thank you for teaching me."

Audrey didn't reply. She let a silence settle between them, around them, as if there was something she couldn't voice. Something with weight beyond that of a driving lesson. It settled, rested heavily; it brought tears to the beautiful eyes, and Ruth knew.

"Velma," Ruth said softly.

Audrey closed her eyes, and Ruth leaned forward to kiss away a tear. "Yes," Audrey replied, "Velma."

The unmistakable squeak of the screen door captured their attention, and Ruth turned to see Mrs. Welly standing in the open doorway.

"I've been thanking the good Lord since the moment I heard the car pull in," she was saying as Ruth exited the car. "Don't know that I ever could've forgiven myself if anything had happened to you girls."

Ruth squeezed around the screen and wrapped her arms around Mrs. Welly's shoulders. "Not a thing to worry about. Audrey's a very good driver, and she's going to make one out of me, too. We're just fine."

"Well, I'm not the only one worrying after you," she said "A woman has called twice for you. She said it's important that you call as soon as you can." Ruth motioned for Audrey to follow. "I wrote her number down by the phone."

Ruth rushed through the kitchen to the living room and the phone with one thought in mind. Audrey was right behind her as she found the piece of paper and dialed the number.

"Lillian?" Audrey asked, and received a nod.

The phone picked up on the second ring. "I'm so sorry, Lillian," Ruth began. "I just now got home. Is it Amelia?"

"She's fine," Lillian replied, "but I've been worried that I wouldn't find the right place for her in time. I think she is going to deliver a little early."

154

"How early?"

"This week, maybe three days." Lillian's voice picked up energy. "But I found it. I have a safe place for her. Now we have to find a way to get her there."

"We have it," Ruth said. "A car."

Lillian's voice carried obvious concern. "Whose car, Ruth? Are you sure you can trust him?"

"It'll be my car. It was Mrs. Wellys late husband's car. And before you ask, I am not a good enough driver—yet—but Audrey is a Jim Cracky driver."

There was a hesitation before Lillian said, "I have to be honest with you, I never thought we would find a way—not in time. I don't think I will believe it until it's over and Amelia is actually safe."

"I think we have all had our doubts. But I'm not willing to let doubt, or anything else, get in our way."

"I will be holding my breath a lot." Despite her words, there was a sense of relief in Lillian's voice. "We've got no time, either for spare or for error, now. We'll have to get the timing figured out perfectly. Call me as soon as you are home from work tomorrow, even if it's into the 'lines clear' hours. This is important, too."

"I will. Thank you, Lillian."

"It's happening faster than we thought," Audrey remarked.

"But it *is* happening."

Chapter 26

The variables were daunting. In just over forty-eight hours the exhilaration of a plan coming together had given way to apprehension and *what ifs*.

The trip to Jackson to lay out the plan with Lillian also served as a practice run to know exactly where they would be going and how long it would take. There wouldn't be enough practice time left for Ruth to be the driver. It was clearly Audrey's responsibility, and she welcomed it.

They followed Lillian's directions and picked her up at the back entrance of the hospital, the same door Ruth had used, the same one Amelia would use. The plan continued to emerge as they drove to Lillian's, and finalized as they once again huddled together in her living room.

"Amelia has read your last letter over and over," Lillian directed to Ruth. "And I was able to convince her to leave all your letters with me. I've done my best to encourage her and still be discreet. I was able to use today's examination time to explain that I had found a safe home for her. I told her what I know about the couple, but she is so quiet. I can't figure out what she is thinking, and I'm afraid we aren't going to know if she has the courage to leave until she actually gets in the car."

"I wish I could talk with her face to face," Ruth replied.

Lillian shook her head. "We've done everything we can. It's up to Amelia now."

"If she does get into the car," Audrey asked, "where will we take her?"

"A couple from Canada is going to meet you at a diner on the U.S. side of the bridge." Lillian handed Audrey an envelope. "Here are the directions and how you'll be able to identify them. You both need to wear a yellow daisy so that they can identify you. I will call Robert when I know Amelia's in the car and he will call them."

"What are these people like?" Ruth asked.

"I know very little," she replied. "Only what a trusted source in the nurses' organization was able to learn from another reliable source. There is a small organization in Toronto for victims of rape, their friends and family members, who all support and help each other. This couple's daughter was raped on her way to school. I don't know any more details, but it's enough to trust that Amelia will be safe with them."

"What if the car from the Home shows up before Amelia comes out?" Audrey asked. "Or before we get there?"

"I'm the one who always makes the call to the Home. And since a lot of the doctors don't give a lot of time to the Crittenton girls, they depend on me to let them know when the girls are ready to leave. The normal seven to ten days' stay doesn't apply to Home girls when they give up their babies. So I'll be able to manipulate the timing to a certain extent."

Ruth looked from Lillian to Audrey and back. "There are a lot of things that need to happen just right for this to work."

Lillian reached out and took their hands. "Yes," she said, "there are."

≪ ≪ ≪

Before Ruth realized it, the red-orange orb glowing in the rearview and side mirrors of the car had changed to an occasional glare of light from a following car. The time since leaving Lillian's and beginning their drive home had been consumed with the plan. They talked about it in detail, wondering and worrying aloud.

"Did you ever think that we would be doing this?" Audrey asked.

"Honestly, no," Ruth said. "There certainly is a huge difference between hoping and wishing for something to happen and the responsibility for making it happen."

"You're worried, aren't you?"

Ruth leaned her head against the back of the seat. "Worried about whether I've done enough, if it will all work, worried about letting Amelia down if it doesn't, or what will happen to her if she decides to go home." She turned her head to Audrey's profile silhouetted against the faded gray of the window. The lines were bold and sure, from the straight hold of her head to the strong set of her chin. "You aren't worried, are you?"

"Not about this." She met Ruth's eyes long enough for them to emphasize her concern. "There are things that we will never be able to control, there always will be. Worrying about those things takes energy from what we *can* control. It's been a hard lesson for me to learn, and at times I forget that I've learned it. Guilt creeps in when I forget that the result was from something beyond my control."

"Velma?"

Audrey nodded. "I couldn't do anything to save her from what happened. But by God," she said, and turned her head to speak directly to Ruth, "I'm going to do everything in my power to save Amelia."

Ruth wrapped her hand over Audrey's on the steering wheel. She could feel the wheels on the road and the power of the engine. She felt the control of Audrey's grip, and shared it.

∽ ∽ ∽

The next two days were fraught. Life struggled to continue as normal, while both women knew that a phone call would alter that in an instant. Since it was important to get to and from work and to be able to respond to Lillian's call as quickly as possible, Audrey stayed at Ruth's and drove them to work in the morning.

Realizing that Amelia would be leaving with only what she wore to the hospital, Ruth had used her lunch break the previous day to buy a suitcase and clothes for her. New clothes and a new start—a phone call away.

Audrey added her contribution the night before, tucking an envelope containing the month's money normally invested in government war bonds, into the elastic pocket of the suitcase. A better investment, she was sure.

Yet even with preparation details taken care of, concerns continued to pepper Audrey's thoughts. Had they forgotten anything? Would today be the day Lillian called? How brave could they expect Amelia to be? And the one that prodded her most—was there anything more she could do? She knew why that concern wouldn't leave her, why it resisted all reasoning. If only this time she would be able to answer the unanswerable.

Just as she had done the day before, Audrey hurried from the plant without her usual end-of-day courtesies. Only Nona knew why.

"Keep your train on the track and your passenger safe," she said as Audrey rushed past.

"One day closer to the station," had become Audrey's response.

Ruth was waiting in the restaurant parking lot, and without wasting a minute they went straight to Ruth's, ran inside, and checked the message pad next to the phone.

"She called," exclaimed Ruth, grabbing the phone and dialing Lillian's number. She clasped Audrey's hand as she waited.

"Lillian, it's Ruth," she began as soon as she heard Lillian's voice. "Did she deliver? Is she all right?"

"Yes and yes. Amelia delivered late last night, and she is fine. I was with her all the way through and everything went well. I'm sure that you and Susan sharing your experiences with her was a tremendous help. She knew what to expect and she seemed much more calm than I expected."

"Oh, I am so relieved," Ruth said, nodding at Audrey and squeezing her hand. "And how does she seem otherwise?"

"She asked two questions. If her uncle would be able to find her, and if she would ever be able to see her mother and father again."

"I've been worried about that last one."

"Regardless of their deficiencies, they are still her parents," Lillian replied. "And she is still a child."

"Yes," Ruth said. "Something we can't change no matter how much we wish we could."

"What we *can* do is give her every chance possible and hope for the best. And that's what we're doing." Lillian's voice had that same reassurance Ruth had counted on herself not long ago. Now she was counting on it once again. "The Home likes to pick the girls up early on the fifth day," Lillian continued, "but I'm going to have her ready early evening on the fourth day. I'll tell them that she is doing exceptionally well, which she is, and that I think it will be better for her emotionally to be back in a more social environment. That way you two won't have to worry about taking time from work. There is no sense in jeopardizing your jobs if we can avoid it."

"Audrey will be relieved," Ruth said. "I was prepared with an excuse if needed, but it would have been more difficult for her."

"Expect a call around six o'clock on Friday if all goes well."

"Yes, we'll be ready. Thank you, Lillian."

Audrey had no chance to voice her questions. Ruth excitedly offered up everything Lillian had told her. They had known how it was to happen, waited impatiently, and now they knew the when. The expression on Audrey's face, lifted brows and an easy smile, said everything that Ruth was feeling—relieved, hopeful, and anxious.

Audrey glanced at the dining-room window and the soft glow of the sun low in the sky. "We have time before dark," she said. "How about another driving session?"

"You know, there will come a time when you won't have to ask."

Chapter 27

Sharing, they found, made angst bearable. They shared driving sessions, rides to work, dinners, and nights at Ruth's.

The little brass fan sitting atop the bureau ushered the cool night air in through the open bedroom window. Audrey pushed a pillow behind her back against the ornate mahogany headboard and pulled her nightgown over her knees.

Ruth padded down the hallway from the bathroom and closed the bedroom door behind her. "What a lovely sight you are." She added a coy smile as she stuffed her dirty clothes into the bag hanging on the closet knob.

"It just now occurred to me," Audrey said, "I'm about to help kidnap a girl and I don't even know what she looks like."

"We're providing safe passage," Ruth replied, opening the bottom drawer of the bureau. She retrieved a large pad of paper and slipped onto the bed next to Audrey. "Here," she said, flipping through the pages, "this is Amelia." The pencil rendering was of a slender young girl, her head at a gentle tilt, eyes bright and receptive. "This is how I'll always see her, the way she would listen whenever Susan and I would talk. I don't know if it mattered much to her what we were saying as much as she craved the time that was spent specially with her."

"You did this?" Audrey said, more as a statement than a question. "This makes me feel like I know her now." She looked from the drawing to Ruth. "You are so talented. It's beautiful, Ruth. Are there others? Can I see them?"

"I'll let you guess who they are," she replied, turning to the beginning of the pad.

From the stories and descriptions Ruth had offered over the past months, they were easy guesses. Susan and Amelia, the view from Ruth's window, her parents, and Lillian. Audrey pointed her finger sharply at the next picture. "Now this is even more severe than I had imagined," she said. "This has to be the house mother."

"Mrs. Stranton. Then I believe I did her justice," Ruth added with a raise of her eyebrows. "Our most difficult task—for me and Susan—was to undo the negatives that that woman forced on Amelia."

"No wonder she relies on you so much." She held Ruth's eyes for seconds longer as if there was more she wanted to say, but added only, "No wonder." She brought her focus back to the sketches and turned the page. With a smile and a shake of her head, she said, "This is incredible. How did you do this from memory?"

"Do you have any idea how many times you sat there reading the paper between bites of your dinner, and looking up at me like that when I came to the table?"

"Do you have any idea how much I love you?"

Ruth leaned over and pressed her lips to Audrey's—warm with a gentle parting. "No," she whispered, lifting her head, "I'm afraid I have no idea."

The corners of Audrey's lips curled upward, and she pulled Ruth against her chest. "Then I will have to show you."

Chapter 28

The adrenaline surged to a level Audrey had not felt before. Her legs quivered uncharacteristically, even as she brought the car to a stop in The Bomber parking lot.

Ruth, waiting outside the door and no doubt just as anxious, jumped into the passenger seat. Her eyes wide with anticipation, she grabbed Audrey's hand and squeezed it tightly. "Keep the train on the rail and our passenger safe," she said.

"From Nona," Audrey replied.

"And her Moses," Ruth added. "Here we go."

The drive to Jackson was devoid of conversation. It had all been said. What was left was to do their part. The rest was out of their hands.

Audrey checked her watch. Exactly 7:15 when she pulled into the parking lot at the back of the hospital. She stopped short of the spot close to the door Lillian had indicated so that she could pull her hair up onto her head and cover it with Mr. Welly's brown hat, the topper to his suit that she had borrowed from the closet. Ruth covered her tightly pinned bun with a black hat that had a large brim, much like Mrs. Stranton's.

"Good?" Ruth asked.

"Good enough."

With a deep breath Audrey pulled the car across the lot and into place. Maintenance trucks and staff cars lined one end of the building, and trash containers were lined up against the wall on the other side of the entrance. Ruth pulled the brim of the hat farther down over her forehead as two hospital workers emerged from the door to deposit trash into the containers. The same door, Audrey realized, that her Ruth had been expected to use, the same one Amelia would use. In and out with no more respect than was given to the soiled and discarded. She looked at the woman she loved, her profile softened in shadow, and vowed to do all she could to be sure Ruth knew her worth. The one thing she wanted more than anything else. The other was for Amelia to walk through that door.

Audrey looked again at her watch. 7:25. She was about to say something when the door opened again. She leaned forward in anticipation, but it was a janitor emptying a mop bucket in the gravel.

Ruth let out an audible breath, and "False alarm."

"I'm getting worried," Audrey said. "Do you think someone suspected the car wasn't from the Home and wouldn't let her come out?"

"The car at the Home is a black Ford. No one seemed to pay much attention before. Lillian just told me the car was here and I went out the door on my own."

The door opened again, just a crack, then closed. Another ten minutes went by. It was more than Audrey could take. In a flash, Velma was in her thoughts, laughing and tipping her head back under the flow of the fountain, turning and coaxing and splashing with delight. Her Velma, never to be herself again. "I'm not going to let this happen again," she said aloud.

"What?"

"She doesn't know how bad it can be. She's more afraid of the unknown than the abuse she knows." Audrey grabbed the handle and opened the car door. "I have to go get her."

Ruth grabbed Audrey's arm to stop her. "Wait. If she doesn't want to come with us, you can't physically force her. Someone will call the police."

"I have to try. Maybe I can find Lillian." She pulled her arm free and stepped from the car as a frail, frightened girl emerged from the door.

"There she is!" Ruth said. "It's Amelia."

Audrey slipped back behind the wheel, and Ruth opened her door to motion for Amelia to hurry. She opened the back door of the car, ushered Amelia in, and followed her into the back seat. "Go," she directed, "go." She wrapped her arms around the girl's thin frame and held her close. "Oh, Amelia, I've been so worried. Are you all right?"

Her voice was light, barely above a whisper. "Yes, I am now."

"You are going to be safe now, Amelia," Audrey emphasized, glancing into the rearview mirror. "That's a promise."

"And if there is one thing I know for sure about this woman—" Ruth placed her hand on Audrey's shoulder"—it's that you can count on her word. And her heart is bigger than the B-24s she builds."

"Nurse Lillian told me nice things about you. Thank you, Audrey. And you, Ruth. What would I ever do without you?"

"There are a lot of people who care about you," Ruth said.

"But I don't understand why," Amelia replied. "They don't even know me."

"Nurse Lillian and I know you. And the people who know us experience the same fears, question the same injustices, and they want the same chance for happiness. And not just for themselves, but for others, too. For you."

"How am I ever going to be able to thank everyone?"

"By letting your wings grow, even wider and more beautiful than mine, so that you can soar wherever you want and be whoever you want to be. Honey, you can be a wife and a mother if *you* choose to be. You can be a teacher or a nurse, or own your own business someday. There are women doctors, and women pilots, Amelia, soaring the skies just like men do. Let your soul be free to dream and to plan. That's how you can thank us."

"Do I have to start tonight? Can't I be with you for a while?"

"I wish you could. I miss you. There's so much I want to talk with you about. But they know at the Home that you are gone by now. If they catch us, we'll be arrested for kidnapping. We have to keep to the plan, Amelia."

From her expression it was clear. "Oh, no, I didn't know. I would never want you to get in trouble for me."

"That's why we couldn't tell you. We didn't want you to worry about us." But Amelia's frown persisted. "We're going to be fine, really. The most dangerous part is almost over."

⤳ ⤳ ⤳

The car pulled into the usual spot behind the hospital. Mrs. Stranton stared straight ahead beneath the large black rim of her hat. She was waiting in the usual silence for Amelia, today's girl, to emerge from the back door. But something wasn't usual tonight. Fifteen minutes and no one checking from the back door to see if the car was there.

Mrs. Stranton checked her watch. "Joseph," she said, "go see what is holding her up."

He left the car and checked the hallway just inside the door where the girls were normally left, waiting in a wheelchair for the car to arrive. He returned to Mrs. Stranton and announced, "She's not there."

"What?"

"The wheelchair is in the hallway, but the girl isn't there."

"Well, this is unacceptable," she replied. "They're supposed to make sure that she's ready before they call us." Reluctantly she left the car. "Never had to go get a girl," she muttered. "Come on, Joseph."

They searched the hallway, lined with laundry carts and mop buckets, and the bathroom. Mrs. Stranton was visibly frustrated, her face flushed as she marched through the double doors to the main floor and up to the nurses' station.

"Mrs. Stranton from the Crittenton Home," she said. "I need to talk with Lillian Barton."

The nurse behind the desk replied, "She's just down the hall, I'll get her."

Minutes went by, enough to touch the ragged edge of Mrs. Stranton's patience. She stood with her hands on her hips and stared down the hall.

Joseph broke the silence. "Maybe something happened and they have to keep her longer." His attempt to ease her aggravation had no outward effect. Past experience convinced him not to try again.

"I will be having a talk with Mr. Burgess," she said, still staring straight ahead. "Someone needs to answer for this." She turned to look for a staff member when Joseph stopped her.

"Mrs. Barton is coming," he said.

"Well," Mrs. Stranton began the moment the nurse was in earshot, "just what is going on? We have been waiting," she checked her watch, "for over thirty minutes. Why isn't our girl ready?"

Thirty minutes, Lillian thought, not quite enough time but a good start. Mrs. Stranton's reaction was exactly as she had expected, and now her response was well-rehearsed. "She *was* ready, right on time. I left her with an orderly right where the girls always wait." Not a bit of a lie.

Mrs. Stranton's voice rose a pitch. "She's not there. And she's not in the hallway anywhere, or in the bathroom. Where is she?"

"Let me find the orderly," Lillian replied.

Joseph tried his theory once more. "Would she have been taken back to her room if she wasn't feeling well?"

"She would have been taken to the ER temporarily to have a doctor check her. I'll run down to the ER first."

"I'm not waiting here another minute," Mrs. Stranton said. "I'm coming with you."

She walked, brisk and determined, alongside Lillian until they reached the ER, and waited outside the swinging doors while Lillian looked for Amelia. No long wait this time as Lillian returned quickly with her next move.

"No, she wasn't brought here," she reported. "But the orderly is on his way down to meet us."

Mrs. Stranton's voice took on a biting edge. "How do you just misplace a patient?"

"I can tell you," Lillian said, "that it has never happened in the time that I have been here. And there may be a simple explanation. Let's not worry just yet."

Not yet, not until the young man running down the hall toward them nervously answered the all-important question. "Daniel," Lillian began, "the young girl I left you with in the back hallway, do you know where she is?"

He smiled as though his answer was about to ease the obvious tension facing him. "Oh, yes," he said, "the car came just as you said it would and I watched to be sure that she got in safely."

"A car," Mrs. Stranton almost shouted. "What car?"

"The black Ford," he said, his eyes wide, "parked near the building where you showed me, Mrs. Barton."

"She's gone?" Mrs. Stranton's face was flushed a bright red, her cheeks quivered. "She got into someone else's car and she's gone?"

Lillian held her silence and calculated the time in her head. If all was going well, they should be about halfway to their destination.

"Call the police, Joseph," Mrs. Stranton demanded.

◈ ◈ ◈

Lillian watched an uncomfortable Mrs. Stranton describe Amelia to the police sergeant. Her hands shook as she used them to indicate Amelia's height and size. Her cheeks quivered as she spoke. This was obviously not something she had anticipated, nor had she prepared to deal with it.

The orderly gave his description of the car— thankfully no standout from Mr. Ford's manufacturing back yard—and an estimate of when everything occurred, with a give or take of fifteen minutes. Just the amount of time the Home's car would have comfortably taken for the trip to the hospital after the phone call. Lillian counted on Mrs. Stranton finding no issue with the timing.

She watched the older woman—no indication yet, only a level of discomfort that made Lillian wish that she hadn't needed to put her through this. As much as she disagreed with the woman's philosophies and methods, Mrs. Stranton was not in a position to do anything except follow the law. It was painful to watch. And Lillian was guiltily grateful that she wasn't the one having to break the news to Amelia's family.

"We'll be dispatching cars to canvas the immediate area and a distance in all directions that they may be traveling," the sergeant informed them. "And we'll get the description out to the precincts beyond that." He sent another officer out to the patrol car to radio the information, and directed his question once again to Mrs. Stranton. "Now, is there a possibility that the girl's family came to pick her up?"

"No," she replied. "I never notify the families until we have the girls back at the Home."

He directed his next question to Lillian. "Well, then, did she make any phone calls from the hospital?"

"No, only hospital personnel have phone access."

"And did she have any visitors?"

"No, no one."

"Any friends visit her at the Home?" he asked Mrs. Stranton.

"No one is allowed to visit, not even family," she replied.

"Any friends that she may have been in contact with, letters, phone calls?"

Lillian knew what he suspected. The timing of a car showing up before the Home car pointed to Amelia running away, not to a kidnapping. The letters were safely hidden, but was there any other way that they could prove Ruth's involvement?

Mrs. Stranton's first response was "No." But then she added, "There were two girls she was close with while they were at the Home."

"I'll need their names," he said. "She may have said something to them that will help."

Or they might be accomplices. Lillian offered a silent prayer that the girls were far enough away, close enough to their destination to be safe. For now it was all she could do—pray and wait for Robert's phone call.

∽ ∽ ∽

"Have you met them," Amelia asked. "The people who want me to live with them?"

"No. We know as much as Nurse Lillian told you. We will be meeting them together, and we'll have some time to talk with them. You can ask any questions you want."

The sound of their voices behind her, encouraging, loving tones, lifted away Audrey's angst and worry. She breathed in the hope and promise of Ruth's words and smiled at the gentle emergence of freedom. Amelia was almost free. And something surging through Audrey made her want to shout it to the world, to pound the steering wheel in defiance, to run and twirl and fling her arms wide, and celebrate. She wanted to take Velma's face in her hands and whisper, "For you."

Nothing, absolutely nothing, could take this from her. This happiness, this sense of fulfillment, this—redemption. It was so real now. Not a wish pleaded skyward with no hope of deliverance. It was here, right now, lifting the weight of years. She basked in the feeling, letting it carry her until a red flashing glow in the rearview mirror sent an electric bolt through it.

"Quick," her voice jumped with alarm, "get down on the floor. Now."

With a quick glance out the back window it was clear why. Ruth grabbed Amelia and they dropped to the floor. They could hear a siren now in the distance, gradually growing louder.

Audrey heard Ruth's voice, low from behind. "Were you going too fast?" There didn't seem enough breath to answer. "No," Audrey managed, "Thirty-two."

"Stay as flat as you can," Ruth directed at Amelia, placing the big black hat on the flat of the girl's back. "And keep your head down." Her own hope for concealment was the dark shoulder wrap she had chosen to mimic Mrs. Stanton's.

"No, no," Audrey's whisper was barely audible above her own heartbeat. "Don't let this happen. Please, don't let this happen."

The scream of the siren grew louder and the flashes of red gained ground, closing the distance quickly. Her heartbeat hammering in her throat, Audrey slowed the car to a crawl and pulled to the side of the road. "Stay down," she said sharply. "And pray."

The car rolled to a stop. Audrey gripped the wheel tightly and looked straight ahead. She closed her eyes and tried to force her fear into calm. How do I answer? Where am I going? Whose car is this? What if he sees them? "Breathe," she whispered, and drew in air, shakily.

Audrey opened her eyes and chanced a look into the mirror. The interior of the car illuminated red and the siren screamed its crescendo. The police car raced past them. She stared in disbelief as she watched the car speed away, then dropped her head to the steering wheel with a long, audible exhale in relief. She leaned her head back against the seat and drew a deep, full breath that lifted her, light as air, above her fear.

"It's okay," she whispered. Then louder, "It's okay. It's all clear. You can get up now."

Ruth poked her head cautiously above the back of the driver's seat. "What was it?"

"I don't know," Audrey replied with a turn of her head. "Only that it's not us. Are you both okay?"

Ruth looked at Amelia, settling again next to her on the seat. "Except for a bit of a scare," she said.

Amelia's voice was distinctively light. "What if they had stopped us, Audrey? What would you have said?"

Audrey lowered her voice to a husky tone reminiscent of a barely legal young man. "John Tower, sir, driving the car back to my big brother."

"Maybe," Ruth said, "with the suit and hat. But Jack's little brother? What if he wanted to follow you to Jack's?"

"Pray he doesn't see you two, and that Jack's not home."

"We ducked one," Ruth replied with a sigh of relief.

Amelia's light, timid voice took on an unusual energy. "We're really on the run, aren't we?"

As she pulled the car back onto the road, Audrey smiled and replied. "We are indeed."

∽ ∽ ∽

Audrey stopped the car near the edge of the parking lot of the State Side Diner. Quickly she shed the suit and fedora, struggled out of the trousers, and wiggled into a skirt. A transformation suitable for meeting Amelia's new family. Ruth handed her a yellow daisy and they both wound the flowers into their hair.

"Come on," Ruth said. She smiled and took Amelia's hand as they exited the car. "This is the good part."

The diner was a bustle of activity. Waitresses glided between tables and booths, and the air was filled with friendly chatter and tempting aromas. As they promised, Mr. and Mrs. Samuels had claimed an early booth and were waiting for Amelia's arrival.

"There they are," Ruth said, still holding Amelia's hand. "Tan floppy hat with a daisy."

It was the first thing they noticed, of course, the identifying marker, but the second thing Audrey noticed was more important. She saw joy, pure and untethered, in the eyes and the smile of Mrs. Samuels. The woman seemed to twinkle with joy. Throughout the introductions and the initial conversation, Audrey watched, gathering the unspoken and waiting for anything that would counter what their words were saying. But there was nothing, from either of them. Audrey watched Mr. Samuels closely for obvious reasons. In his soft blue eyes she saw the glimmer of pride whenever his wife spoke. He leaned forward, listening intently when others spoke, and asked the questions of Amelia that Audrey hoped any parent would ask. *How do you like school? What is your favorite subject? What is one of your favorite things to do?* Audrey was convinced: The Samuels' home was the right place for Amelia.

"Our daughter, Betsy, is so excited to meet you, Amelia," Mrs. Samuels was saying. "She's been working for a dentist in town. She started out keeping his books, but she's been learning everything she can and now he wants her to go to school so that he will be able to hire her as his assistant. She made us promise to bring you to the office so that she can show you around. And she'll be so proud to show you her own room above the office. You are all she has talked about for the past week."

"Does she make her own money? Is it hers to keep?" Amelia asked.

"It's hers, she earned it," Mr. Samuels said. "She's a very responsible girl, pays her bills first, puts money away in savings—"

"And spends too much money on presents for her parents," Mrs. Samuels added with a wink. "But that is all I can fault her for."

"Can I meet her tomorrow?" asked Amelia.

"If you have the energy, that's the first place we will go."

Amelia turned to Ruth, her brow forming a vee above her nose. "Will I ever get to see you again?"

Before the glisten in Amelia's eyes could form into tears, Ruth said, "Of course you will. Remember I have a car now, and Audrey is patiently teaching me to be a good driver. Coming to see you will be my first real road trip." Amelia's face burst into a wide smile. "And meantime, you write me letters as often as you can and tell me about all the wonderful new things in your life. I put Audrey's address in your suitcase, so send them there just in case they come looking for you at my place."

"I will," Amelia promised. "I'll write you every day." She wrapped her arms around Ruth's waist, hugged her tightly, and said softly, "I love you, Ruth."

"I love you, too. And I am over-the-moon happy for you."

Chapter 29

The goodbyes were teary, poignant, but not the worrisome sadness Audrey had anticipated. It made the trip home a happy prelude to an evening of celebration. And it was only fitting that their celebration include Nona.

They kept their enthusiasm in check so that they wouldn't frighten Mrs. Bailey, and knocked on the side door. Moments later the center of the drape covering the window in the door parted just enough for someone to peer out.

"It's Audrey, Mrs. Bailey, and Ruth."

The door opened to Mrs. Bailey's less than convincing chastising. "Oh, now look what time a night it is, and not a Friday night, either."

"I'm sorry," Audrey replied as the old woman closed the door behind them. "But I have exciting news and I can't wait to tell Nona."

"Come on, then," she said. "Nona's reading her books in the dining room."

The disruption brought Nona to the kitchen, and as soon as Audrey saw her she exclaimed, "We did it, Nona. We did it!"

"I never doubted that you would. Not once," she said.

Audrey wrapped her arms around Nona and twirled her around and around and around. "We did it! We did it! We did it!"

Ruth caught Nona's eyes as the last twirl came to a dizzying stop. "Thank you," Ruth said.

"No," Nona replied. "You two did all the work and took all the risk."

"Well, I suppose," Mrs. Bailey muttered, and moved toward the icebox, "whatever it is you girls did, you'll be wantin' some ice tea. Go on now, get yourselves settled."

Audrey moved quickly to her side. "I'll help you." It hadn't taken long for her to love this old woman—her understated sense of humor, her subtle scrutiny, and ultimately, her acceptance of a slightly out-of-bounds white girl. The love, Audrey suspected, was mutual.

They delivered the tray of refreshments to the midst of the enthusiastic conversation at the dining table. Mrs. Bailey took her opportunity at the first lull. "Now, who's gonna tell me what you did before the police come knockin' on my door?"

A bit closer to the truth than she could know, Audrey thought, as all eyes centered on Nona. She would have to decide what was appropriate.

"We," Nona began, making eye contact all around, "saved a young girl from a dangerous situation." A silence followed. No one seemed willing to add anything further.

Mrs. Bailey looked from one to another, then settled on Nona and broke the silence. "You are a terrible storyteller." No one even tried to contain their laughter. Even Nona, the target at the end of the barb, laughed at the obvious. "Anyone gonna tell me the story," Mrs. Bailey tried again, "or am I supposed to wait and read it in the newspaper?"

This time everyone's attention shifted to Ruth. "Nona doesn't want to get us in trouble," she began. "A young girl that I know was violated by a family member and was sent to the Crittenton Home. Her family thinks that she lied about how it happened and threatened to institutionalize her if she continued her accusation. She would have been sent back into a situation where she no doubt would have been violated again. So we made sure that wouldn't happen."

Mrs. Bailey was captivated, as if she were visualizing the story of a favorite radio program. "How did you do it?"

"We picked her up from the hospital and took her to a family who will take her in and keep her safe."

"Just you two," Mrs. Bailey said, "driving a car yourself."

"It's parked in front of your house right now."

"Mmm, mm," she said, "and you were worried about tellin' this old girl. You were, weren't you?"

"We could go to jail for this," Ruth offered. "We have to be careful."

Mrs. Bailey squared up rounded shoulders and pressed back hard against the chair back. "Humph," she said, indignation pushing her chin down to her neck and lowering her focus to something short of the table. "Well," her focus raised and narrowed on Nona, "let me ask you: Forty years ago, if he'd been caught, what would have happened to a young Negro boy who regularly snuck behind the barn to kiss the daughter of his white employer?"

Nona's eyes widened. "He would have been lynched."

"As fast as they could get a rope over the closest tree branch," Mrs. Bailey said with a nod. "And if there was a young Negro girl working there, too, who diverted the mother's attention so that she wouldn't know her daughter was out of the house—what would have happened to *her*?"

Nona stared into the old woman's eyes. "She was a conspirator."

Mrs. Bailey nodded. "Lynched, right alongside that boy." She nodded again. "Right alongside."

Nona's eyes never left Mrs. Bailey's. "It was you."

Of course it was, Audrey thought. Born and raised in a time ripe with risk. And *we* question her understanding of it? A depth of understanding that we can only hope to fathom. Did I have any real idea of risk and consequence at that age? Would I have had the same courage then? "Who was he?" she asked.

"A silly boy who was crazy in love," she replied. "No sense in that boy's head at all. One word from that white girl, one slip from me . . ."

"But why did you help him?" Ruth asked.

Her eyes, dark liquid, seemed to scan time. Maybe searching for a way to explain the unexplainable. But she tried. "You know, that wasn't a question that ever got asked. There was always enough holding us back, enough noes and taboos." She looked directly at Nona. "So when you see a chance, something that's not supposed to be there, you don't ask why." She finished with a quick nod of her head.

Nona smiled and nodded in return.

"So," Mrs. Bailey added, and turned her attention to Audrey and Ruth. "This old girl knows a little about risk. She'll keep your secret."

Chapter 30

The notices, with a not-that-close sketch of of Amelia, were distributed in communities along major roads leaving the Jackson area. There was one stuck on the front window of The Bomber, a reminder to Ruth every day that things were not over. Whether she was a runaway or a kidnap victim, a young girl was missing. Every day for the past three days there had been notices in the newspapers and spots on the radio. The attention didn't rise to the level of the Lindbergh kidnapping, but it was enough to keep Ruth on edge.

They had taken Lillian's warning seriously—that the police had Ruth's name and that she must be prepared for them to find her, and for their questions. And they *were* prepared—for that, and more.

Ruth worried about Audrey being implicated, but it only made sense for the car to be kept at Audrey's. It certainly could not be sitting in Mrs. Welly's driveway, they couldn't have the police questioning her about it. It seemed that the best scenario was for them each to stay at their own place and to see each other only at the restaurant. They had thought it out carefully, thoroughly. Ruth was prepared. At least, she thought she was.

Mrs. Welly had joined the ladies at Mrs. Bradley's to write Victory letters to the soldiers. What would once have been welcome—an evening alone—now felt lonely and empty. She wondered if nights away from each other felt as empty for Audrey. Nights together had quickly defined their needs, their desires, blending them into a beautiful, heated blur. They depended on those nights, tucked away from the world, stripped of pretense. They bared their bodies and their souls as naturally as a river caressing its destined path. Life was as it should be in their tiny space in the world.

Ruth wandered into the kitchen for the second time, stood there for a moment, and left again without getting anything to eat. She closed the book she'd been trying to read, left it on the dining table, and settled herself on the davenport in the living room. With a click of the radio knob she attempted to cut the unnerving silence in the house. There was, she decided, a difference between quiet silence and lonely silence. And she had realized something else as well. The freedom she had been seeking from restriction and expectation, the freedom that she had found, breathed its fullest, deepest breath when she shared it with Audrey. Ruth leaned her head against the back of the davenport and took a long, deep breath. There was no feeling like it.

The rapping on the front door jarred her from her thoughts. She jumped up from the davenport, her heart pounding hard. A quick look between the drapes confirmed her fear. She had gone over the possible questions with Audrey, practiced the answers, practiced *how* to answer. She was prepared, but still her hand shook as she reached for the doorknob. Not prepared for the shallow, shaky breaths as she opened the door. And definitely not for the tremor in her legs that threatened to fold them beneath her. Facing her was a State Police officer.

"Are you Ruth Evans?" he asked.

"Yes," Ruth replied, and then the reply she had decided on if she was alone. "Is Mrs. Welly all right?"

Her worried tone and wide eyes softened his stern expression. "Mrs. Welly?"

"My landlady, Edna Welly, is she okay?"

"Oh," he said. "I didn't mean to worry you. I'm not here about your landlady. Are you Ruth Evans?"

"Yes," she said, still with a concerned look. "What's this about?"

"I need to ask you some questions. May I come in?"

"Yes," she replied, "of course."

He removed his cap and stepped inside. Ruth struggled to slow her breathing as the officer retrieved a small pad of paper and pencil from his shirt pocket.

"Do you know a young girl named Amelia Garrett?" he began.

"Yes," she said, allowing the concern to return to her voice.

"How do you know Amelia?"

She hated the flush creeping over her face, the lack of control to stop it—betrayal of an embarrassment she thought she had left behind. "We were at the Crittenton Home in Jackson during the same time." Then the tactic Audrey had suggested. "Is something wrong? Has something happened to Amelia?"

"We're trying to locate her," he said. "When was the last time you saw her?"

And now the lies, the ones she had practiced with Audrey. Don't hesitate, don't avoid eye contact. "I said goodbye to her at the Home after I delivered. She wasn't due for a few more months." *As close to the truth as she could keep it.* "She should have just delivered, I think." Stop talking. Just answer his questions.

"Were you close to Amelia when you were at the Home?"

He's going to know the answer to that from Mrs. Stranton. "Yes. She was so young and so scared that some of us older girls tried to look after her."

"Did she tell you about a boyfriend?"

"No, she was too shy to talk about personal things."

"Was there anything she said that would make you think that she wanted to run away from her family?"

Ruth shook her head and kept eye contact. "No."

"Has she called or written to you?"

"No," Ruth replied. "I hope she is all right."

"Do you have any idea where she might be or who else she may have contacted?"

Another shake of her head. "No." The acid in her stomach began to burn. *He thinks that she ran away. Isn't that best? No criminal to look for in a kidnapping, only a boyfriend who will be in a load of trouble if found. Not two conniving women who made sure she ran away. Deep breath, deep breath. This is going to be okay.*

"You say that Amelia hasn't contacted you," he tried again and locked his eyes directly on Ruth's.

"No," she said, trying hard to keep from pulling her eyes away from the cool scrutiny. "I mean yes, she hasn't." *How many more lies? How many more ways can he reword the same questions? He's looking for a slipup. Of course he is.*

He was unrelenting. "And you didn't remember her saying anything about not wanting to go back home or wanting to be with her boyfriend? A name she may have mentioned in passing?"

Don't hesitate. "No, I never heard her say anything like that." *Not exactly a lie, is it? Reading it instead of hearing it? Did it really matter anymore?*

Her stomach burned, the acid roiled. She was sure that she would throw up before he left. The bitterness bubbled up to her throat. She swallowed to stop it.

The officer looked up from his pad. "If she contacts you," he said as if he knew she would, "you need to call us." He tore a piece of paper from the pad and handed it to Ruth. "If you hear *anything*," he insisted, "call."

"Yes, of course," she replied. Anything, she'd say anything right now if it would make him leave. She watched, her breath short of exhale as he turned toward the door. Her heart spiked a beat when he hesitated, the screen door half open, and turned to face her again. He looked at her as if there was one more question he should ask. Ruth refused to exhale.

"Good night, ma'am," he said with a nod and left.

Her relief was audible. She locked the door and leaned her back against it. Not until she heard the car pull away did she scratch out a note and leave it on the table for Mrs. Welly. Getting out of the house, shedding the worry was her only thought. Upstairs she gathered her toiletries and makeup and packed them with a clean uniform in her overnight bag. It wasn't until she grasped the knob of the side door that a thought stopped her. What if the police were waiting to see if she would leave, to see if she did indeed know where Amelia was? More than anything she just wanted to be with Audrey, to say what she needed to say, to hear what she needed to hear—safe, absorbing Audrey's strength and her confidence. But it would have to wait, an hour, maybe more.

৯৯ ৯৯ ৯৯

More it was, Ruth erring on the side of caution. It was dark and late before she was able to feel the strength of Audrey's arms around her.

"You're shaking," Audrey said, holding Ruth tightly and pressing her cheek to the sleek, dark hair pulled tight over Ruth's ear.

"Am I?" Ruth replied.

"You are. Are you okay?" She pulled away to look into Ruth's eyes. "Did he ask the questions we thought he would?"

Ruth nodded. "Over and over," she said, "as if he knew I was lying, as if by asking them a little differently he would get the truth."

"That's what he is trained to do. But you stuck to your answers, didn't you?" Ruth nodded. "Then everything's going to be fine. Come on and sit down, it's going to be fine." She took Ruth's hand and settled next to her on the edge of the bed.

"I never thought it would be so hard to lie like that. I was a wreck, Audrey, and not just emotionally. I was a physical wreck." She shook her head. "I really hate this. I am a terrible liar."

Audrey sat cross-legged on the bed facing Ruth, and took her face in her hands. What she saw in Ruth's eyes confirmed the fear Audrey had only recently been able to override. Not being able to lie, she knew firsthand, was dangerous, emotionally and otherwise.

"It'll get better," Audrey said. "It'll be easier, it will." More a plea than a promise.

"Lying about Amelia? It's over, isn't it?" Ruth asked. "Please tell me it's over."

The feeling punched Audrey in the gut and scared the hell out of her. The eyes she saw weren't Ruth's, the naivety not hers at all, but Velma's. Her worst fear coming true, that Ruth like Velma could not, would not understand that lying would keep them safe.

"Not yet," Audrey replied. "The lies are keeping Amelia safe. Hopefully those lies have done their job and you won't have to worry about the police now. But neither of us are done with lies. Lies are what will keep *us* safe."

"But not like this." Her tone seemed to lack conviction. "Stomach threatening to give up anything it's got, nerves making my hands shake and my legs quiver. Not like that."

"It gets easier, Ruth."

"How many lies does that take? And what does that say about us when we *do* find it easy?"

Ruth's voice now had a conviction that made Audrey uncomfortable. It was clear that the lies necessary to save Amelia were singular, and to Ruth, unavoidable. But other lies, those impending, less imminent—did she see them as avoidable? Those lies Audrey knew were not.

"How ever long it takes," Audrey said. "And it will mean that we're comfortable protecting ourselves." She stood to try to calm the agitation. "It means we know what the risks are if we don't do whatever we have to, to protect who we are."

"So we lie about who we are."

"Yes," Audrey replied. "We lie—about anything that could hurt us, *to* anyone who could hurt us."

Ruth reached out, grasped Audrey's hand to bring her closer. The worry was evident in Audrey's eyes, direct and unwavering. "I don't want to worry you—about me, about us," Ruth said. "Velma will always be a reminder. I will never risk what we have together. I love you, Audrey. More than anything. I'm just afraid of giving up too much of who we are."

"Like?"

She pulled Audrey down to sit next to her again. "Like not compromising our independence. I like having my own money. I like driving. I like going anywhere I want without a man. I like working." Ruth gently stroked Audrey's cheek. "I always want to be the woman you fell in love with that day in the restaurant."

Audrey placed her hand over Ruth's and held it to her cheek. "You will be, always. And I want the same things you do."

"Then you can't worry us into a corner. We can't let what happened to Velma make us afraid to live our lives."

"But there are going to be times when we *have* to lie, when we *have* to protect ourselves, even when it goes against everything we believe in."

"So where's the line?" Ruth asked. "Where do the edges of us touch the edges of who we're supposed to be?"

Audrey pulled Ruth to her and buried her face into the warmth of Ruth's neck. "I don't know," she whispered.

Chapter 31

August 1944

Time passed, weeks into months, without normal measure. Routine markers of work schedules, Monopoly and ice cream nights, and paydays were replaced by more important markers. While Audrey and her coworkers were posting amazing production numbers sending a finished bomber out the door at a clip of one every hour, the news reports from the war fronts marked what was beginning to look like a war winding down. That month alone, Allied forces reached north Italy and breached the Gothic Line, Germany's last strategic position there; forced the Japanese into total retreat in India; and liberated Guam to gain control of the Marianas.

It was a wave of high hope, coupled with an emotional high that Audrey would never have predicted—Amelia was safe, and Audrey blessed with a love that had brought her through the fog and the doubt, and filled her days and nights with light and brilliance.

There hadn't been a moment yet when Audrey wondered how long it would last, not a night when she lay alone in fear that it was only a beautiful dream. Her life, her love with Ruth was real, and more than she had thought possible. Now her wish would be for everyone to have such love and happiness fill their lives.

But, of course, it wasn't always possible. Life, with its ebbs and flows, offered only chances. Promises must face challenges unseen, and happiness must weather the seasons.

☙ ☙ ☙

To a person, everyone in the plant knew what the appearance of a Western Union messenger meant. And to a person, they all prayed to whatever God they worshiped that the delivery was not for them. They all waited and watched. Was it their husband, father, brother, friend?

You could almost feel the air being sucked and held from station to station as the messenger made his way past one after another. Workers donning aprons and readying tools watched intently until he passed.

Audrey, too, watched. And when he neared their station she turned her attention to Janice and June. The two women stood frozen in place, averting their eyes as if doing so would make the messenger pass them by. To Audrey it seemed somehow wrong that she could watch without personal worry. Only Nona knew that she feigned whatever worry others saw.

No one moved now as the messenger slowed and stopped. He surveyed the faces of the women, who at this moment were no doubt shouting silent frantic prayers.

"I have a message," he said, not knowing which woman his delivery was about to devastate, "for Mrs. June Baker." He pushed the telegram into the open space before him that no one had wanted to enter.

Before anyone could respond, June's knees buckled and she folded into a heap on the floor.

"I'm sorry," he said, still holding out the telegram.

Janice, with a nervous exhale, took it from him, as Audrey moved quickly to June's aid. She tried to help her to her feet, but June's legs had no strength. Audrey knelt beside her and tightened her arms around the shaking shoulders.

She looked up to see Jack shaking his head sadly. "I'm sorry, June," he said. "We'll get you home. You need to be with your family." With Jack's help they got June to her feet and walked her out to a break table.

Each of the crew touched June's shoulder, offered whatever condolence they could manage, and returned dutifully to the station. Jack took the telegram from Janice and handed it to Audrey. "Stay with her," he said, "until we can get her home. We'll cover."

Covering wasn't first in anyone's thoughts. They would do what they needed to do, that was automatic, an imprint set by rote. Expressed or not, each crew member carried their own concerns and sympathy and relief into the day. Tonight they would do what they could for June.

Right now, though, it was up to Audrey. She began by trying to lay the telegram on June's lap.

"No, no," June said, vigorously shaking her head and pushing the telegram from her lap as if it had burst into flames.

Audrey picked it up. "June," she said softly, "maybe it's notifying you that he's been wounded. You need to know. You've already imagined the worst, reading it—"

"Makes it real," June said, her voice uncharacteristically weak. "I can't lose him." Her eyes, wet with tears, frightened and wide, met Audrey's. "What would I do without him?"

"We don't know that you will have to yet. But if you do, you will do exactly as you have been, taking care of your two boys, taking care of your family and yourself. You've proven you can do that, June. I think you've even surprised yourself as to how well you have done that, haven't you?"

"But it's not right. It's not what I want my life to be." Her tears ran a hard course now down her cheeks, forming dark blue blotches as they landed on the thighs of her jumpsuit.

"I know you don't. But you're strong, June. Stronger than you think you are."

"I don't want to be strong. I want my life back, the way it was before this god awful war."

"But if that isn't possible, you have to find a way to look into those little boys' eyes and make them know that they will be okay. And you will, June, you will."

June dropped her forehead to the palms of her hands. She sobbed silently and Audrey put her arm around her shoulders and drew her close. She gently stroked the back of June's head as she rested against her.

A little while later, June's breathing regained its rhythm and the sobs subsided. Softly, against Audrey's shoulder, she asked, "What does it say?"

Audrey slipped her arms from June and opened the telegram. She read it to herself first so that she could reform the message in her own words.

SAE 89 GOVT = PXX NR WASHINGTON, DC 26 111 A

MRS. JUNE BAKER =
933 HILLTOP STREET =
YPSILANTI, MICHIGAN =

THE ARMY AIR FORCE DEPARTMENT DEEPLY REGRETS TO INFORM YOU THAT YOUR HUS-BAND, DANIEL BAKER FLIGHT OFFICER FIRST CLASS IS MISSING IN ACTION IN THE PERFORM-ANCE OF HIS DUTY AND IN THE SERVICE OF HIS COUNTRY WHEN HIS PLANE WAS SHOT DOWN IN A MISSION OVER NORMANDY, FRANCE. THE DEPARTMENT EXTENDS TO YOU ITS SINCEREST SYMPATHY AND ASSURES YOU IF FURTHER DETAILS ARE RECEIVED YOU WILL BE NOTIFIED IMMEDIATELY.

LT. COL. ROBERT H. TERRILL
COMMANDING OFFICER
EIGHTH AIR FORCE

Audrey took a slow breath, looked into June's waiting eyes and said calmly, "He's missing, June. His plane was shot down over Normandy, France."

"Oh, God!" She clasped her hands to her head. "Oh, God."

"It means there's hope." Audrey forced June to look at her. "For now there's hope. He could have parachuted out. You know they won't leave him behind, even if he's captured. You know that."

"Yes," June replied, her eyes finally focusing. "Yes, he's a tough soldier, he's smart. They'll find him. They will."

Audrey offered a reserved smile, an attempt to comfort, to affirm what she honestly could not in her own mind. She had no idea of the statistics for MIAs coming home alive, but she feared that they weren't favorable. She feared that for June.

Not knowing what more she could say or do to ease June's fear and her pain, Audrey was relieved when a soldier appeared and offered his hand to June. Like an obedient child she took it and then his arm. "I'll take you home," he said.

ော ော ော

But the worry didn't stop with June, and the world turning ass-end-up for her. Like most everyone, Audrey was attuned to the rumors, hints that the war was winding down, which was both wonderful and unsettling all at the same time. The end of the war would mean lives would be spared, the world stabilized and safer. Rationing would end and industry would move from supplying the war effort to making products available and lives easier for everyone. But it was unlikely that a plant the magnitude of Willow Run and its own army of work-ers would have a purpose in peace to match the need in war. There were a number of rumors about the plant's future. Ford might sell it, or part of it, to the highest bidder. He might convert it into a man-ufacturing plant. Or the government might take it over as a military base.

More than a rumor, though, was the fact that thousands of military men would be returning home to a civilian life once again. And when they did, they would need jobs, jobs right now being held by women. Thousands of women, many working since the beginning of the war, now earned their own money, had skills and knowledge in industry that they wouldn't have otherwise, and an independence few would have imagined previously. What would happen to them once they were no longer needed?

Many, of course, welcomed the chance to return to the life they had before the war. For those whose husbands and boyfriends came home healthy and able to work, life would be what they wanted. But what about women like June, needing to provide , needing to continue working? Alone for who knows how long? And for those who wanted to work, those who would always be self-sufficient, independent, in need of good jobs and a good wage—what of them?

The end of the war offered a lot of unanswered questions and an uncertain future for Audrey.

Chapter 32

Uneventful was certainly not a word used to describe most days since the war began. Normal, the expected and accepted, had been redefined. The world, broken into game pieces, had been shaken and tossed down to settle in an unexpected arrangement. A new norm, at least for now.

But since the events surrounding Amelia's rescue, Ruth's days could realistically qualify as uneventful. They had become wonderfully routine. Work was tiring and rewarding. Love was breathless and full, calming and sure. No surprises, no challenges. Until today.

Lillian Barton's phone call wasn't unusual, holiday cards, occasional letters and phone calls were common. This one's message, though, was not. At the end of the conversation Lillian said something that would disrupt the calm. "There's someone I want you and Audrey to meet."

৶ ৶ ৶

Their first sight of her, lying there in the hospital bed, made Ruth want to look away. She had to force herself to look at the battered face, one eye swollen shut and purple, her lips twice their normal size, bloody and split. One arm was wrapped and strapped tightly across her chest.

Ruth and Audrey stood in the hallway outside the room listening to Lillian's explanation. "Her name is Mary," she said. "The official report is that the injuries are a result of a fall down the stairs."

"Official?" Audrey asked.

"She has an injury to her abdomen that surely did not come from a fall," Lillian replied. "And since this is the fourth *accident* resulting in a hospital visit in the last year, I was sure there was more to it, and finally she told me. It's her husband. That's why I called you."

"Why did he do this?" Ruth asked.

"This time?" Lillian said with a tilt of her head. "This time Mary bought a blouse for herself without asking him. Each time the injuries have gotten worse."

Ruth looked again into the room. "So—"

"I think I know what you want," Audrey said, looking directly at Lillian.

"Talk to her," Lillian said.

She didn't need to say more. Ruth caught Audrey's eyes and acknowledged her nod. They entered the room knowing that neither of them would be able to walk away from the challenge ahead.

It wasn't merely pain registering in Mary's eyes. Ruth recognized the fear immediately. She had seen it in Amelia's eyes, heard it in the barely controlled quiver beneath their words. The trust in Lillian, and in two strangers, was born of desperation. That, too, was in Mary's eyes, pleading for an answer, for a solution.

So, they asked the questions and got their answers. *Yes, she made up stories about how she got her injuries; it was embarrassing that she couldn't please her husband. Yes, Nurse Barton had told her that good men do not beat their wives. No, she had no friends she could stay with. Her parents believed that she should be a better wife. She tried to do what her husband wanted, but she was rarely right. Yes, she was afraid of him. Yes, she wanted to leave.*

In the dim solitude of the car Ruth's words took on an unusual magnitude. "What are we going to do?"

Audrey hesitated as the lights of a passing car illuminated her face. "What do you want to do?"

"Something," Ruth replied. "Don't we have to do *something*?"

Audrey pulled her eyes from the road to meet Ruth's in the near darkness. "Lillian expects us to." Her eyes returned to the road. "She didn't have to say it. I'm beginning to think she knows us better than we know ourselves."

"She'll help us," Ruth said. "That is the one thing I am sure of."

"She is sure of something, too. That we can't walk away from this."

❧ ❧ ❧

Had this become their mission, their secret call to arms? Ruth asked herself the question already knowing the answer, already plotting the path forward.

She finished packing her bag with fresh clothes and straightened the folded coverlet at the end of the bed. It was a perfect part of the solution, the room she rarely used, the rent already paid. She would talk with Mrs. Welly tonight. And a job. Her thoughts were jumping ahead so quickly it made her anxious. There was so much to do, so many people to talk to. An old excitement began to edge out worry and apprehension. There was a whole new life out there for Mary. Just as there was for Amelia. A new chance, a new hope. She would feel the excitement of it as soon as she was safe and as soon as fear bowed to the power of independence. One decision, made and trusted, would spur the next, and then the next, until she believed her own strength. That's the way it worked.

Ruth ran down the stairs. There was a mission at hand.

❧ ❧ ❧

Ruth was talking so fast, starting the second that she walked in the door, that Audrey grasped her by the shoulders and met the dancing eyes with a bright smile. "Okay, okay," she said. "Slower, slower, so I can make sense of all this excitement."

"Mary," Ruth replied after a longer than normal breath, "she can stay in my room. I talked with Mrs. Welly and it's fine. The rent is paid, so Mary doesn't have to have money right now. And Martin at The Bomber can take her on part-time. It'll give some of the girls much needed breaks, as long as Mary is okay with an ever-changing schedule." She took another breath.

The look on Ruth's face was the look Audrey needed, the one she had been waiting for and hadn't even realized it. She knew, though, the moment she saw it. There in her eyes, in the pink of her cheeks, and sounding in the passion of her words was the strength—the wonderful, essential strength.

She wrapped her arms around Ruth and hugged her tightly. "Oh, I love you," she said. "Oh, how much I love you."

"You worry way too much, my love." Ruth kissed the side of Audrey's head, her cheek, her neck. "I know why. I do know. But you mustn't worry anymore—about me, about us."

Audrey held her close, felt the promise tighten around her, and vowed never to let go.

"There's going to be only one Velma," Ruth whispered against Audrey's ear. "One Velma to love and cherish. Only one Velma to lose."

Chapter 33

April 1945

It started as a whisper. A cook, tears streaming down his cheeks, whispered the news from the radio in the kitchen. Martin stood for a long moment in the silence, his head bowed, his hand covering his eyes.

As he moved slowly toward the middle of the diner, with no apparent purpose, the customers began to notice. Many stopped talking, held the next bite, watched. He stopped, his arms hanging loosely at his sides, and cleared his throat.

"NBC has just announced," his voice wavered noticeably and tears filled his eyes, spilling uncontrollably down his face. He struggled to continue. "President Roosevelt is dead."

An immediate and collective gasp filled the room, then fell to silence. Shock halted thought, stared into the incomprehensible, prevented any other response. They were, all of them, suddenly riding a ship without a captain—without their longtime leader—the only one many of them had ever known.

The questions and fears beginning to surface were no doubt the same ones filling Ruth's thoughts as she dropped heavily onto the closest stool. As tears coursed down her own cheeks, Ruth asked the questions. What would happen now? Who would lead the troops, the country, keep them safe, win the war? Their plight was left to a Vice President, a man untried and untested. A man the world knew so little about. Who would talk to them now, come into their living rooms to calm their fears and keep the home front solid?

෴ ෴ ෴

They huddled at the table near the radio as they had done every night now for weeks, wondering, like the rest of the nation, who this man, Truman, was. Ruth focused vaguely on the radio, and Audrey wrapped both hands around her coffee cup and stared blankly at the cream-colored contents. They were waiting for a sign that the new President had the reins firmly in hand, that he could and would guide the most powerful forces in the world to victory. It was as if the nation was holding its collective breath until they heard an affirmation or saw the unmistakable bold print headline splashed across the front page of the newspaper. Their voice of reassurance and guidance was silent now, the strong hand at the helm gone. So they waited, night after night, for a sign that they could believe in their new leader.

Then, just as they had wished it, came the voice they needed to hear.

"This is a solemn but glorious hour. I only wish that Franklin D. Roosevelt had lived to witness this day. General Eisenhower informs me that the forces of Germany have surrendered to the United Nations. The flags of freedom fly all over Europe ..."

Audrey met Ruth's eyes, wide with hope and wonder, and motioned her to wait as she started to speak. They listened intently as President Truman continued. He spoke of the sacrifices so many had paid, the terrible price of freedom from evil. And then, what they and an entire nation were wondering: what this meant in the large scheme of things.

"If I could give you a single watchword for the coming months, that word is: work, work, and more work. We must work to finish the war. Our victory is but half won. The West is free, but the East is still in bondage to the treacherous tyranny of the Japanese. When the last Japanese division has surrendered unconditionally, then only will our fighting job be done. . . . The job ahead is no less important, no less urgent, no less difficult than the task which now happily is done. . . . I call upon every American to stick to his post until the last battle is won. Until that day, let no man abandon his post or slacken his effort."

The broadcast continued with the President's official Proclamation, but where the effort stood and what was needed now was clear.

The initial excitement on Ruth's face had tempered. "Do you think it will take as long to win the Eastern part of the war? Look how many years the war has lasted. How many more years, how many more lives is it going to take?"

"We can only hope that it will end soon," Audrey said. "Our campaigns there have been steady since we entered, and now we can concentrate our efforts there, so we *should* have hope."

"Just to think that this war could finally be over—it's a good thought, such a good thought."

Audrey watched the flash of joy return to Ruth's face. "Well, maybe we should celebrate the freedom of half the world."

"There's going to be a lot of that going on, you can be sure," Ruth added. "Do you want to go to the USO?"

"I know most of the crew will be there, but I really don't want to fend off drunken soldiers and plant workers, do you?"

The thought was simultaneous, the natural choice. "Let's go—"

"To Nona's," Ruth finished.

⋙ ⋙ ⋙

Mrs. Bailey met them at the side door. "Did you hear?" she said. "It's a victory day for sure. Makes me wanna dance like I was twenty again."

"You get some music on then," Audrey followed with a smile, "and we will do just that."

Nona's smile was wider and brighter than Audrey had ever seen as she rushed to greet them. "What great news," she said, wrapping Ruth in a tight embrace.

"Worthy of celebration," added Audrey. "So here we are with the makings of white-peach purée and, at least for tonight, no thought of tomorrow."

"What drink is that?" Mrs. Bailey asked. "Sounds too fancy for this simple soul."

"One of the simplest drinks I know," Audrey replied. "Concocted by an Italian and adopted by my father." She placed a bag on the table and reached inside. "Drop this peach into cold champagne and let it fizz. Killer diller," she said, adding a big smile.

Much of the country was indeed celebrating. The big bands dominated the airwaves, signaling hope and the best reason to dance in a very long time.

"It's not something that you forget how to do," Audrey claimed as she pushed the coffee table to the side of the room and took Mrs. Bailey's hand. "Come on, there's nothing like swinging with Benny."

It was contagious, the sense of relief, of reason to be happy, that for now lifted up the weight of war. Ruth grasped Nona's hand and the living room came alive with the steps and swings of the Lindy Hop.

They danced and laughed and shared their joy until Mrs. Bailey collapsed with a giggle onto the davenport. "I haven't had this much fun in years," she said, as she caught her breath. "But you girls are wearing me out."

The girls, though, weren't done. As the harmony of the Andrew Sisters replaced the jazz tempo of Benny Goodman, the three of them sang along to the tribute to the Bugle Boy of Company B. It had been far too long since Audrey had felt the pure joy of song, of letting go of worry, of releasing constraint. And it felt wonderful.

So they kept going, singing along song after song, while Audrey reveled in watching Ruth. Her eyes sparkled and smiled, she bounced with a happy energy, and the vision made Audrey's heart sing. Yes, she could say it—finally, again—she was happy.

Mrs. Bailey clapped, and sang the lyrics that she knew, until Nona and Ruth dropped onto the davenport beside her.

"Oh, you two are so subtle," Audrey said, hands resting on her hips. "You could have just asked me for fresh drinks."

"Please?" Ruth asked.

"For *those* smiles," she replied, "anything."

Anything. It wasn't an exaggeration. To feel the happiness, to see it in their eyes and their smiles, especially Ruth's, she would walk on hot coals, swim an ocean; she would kidnap a girl. And what lit her soul as brightly as the noonday sun was that she knew Ruth felt the same way. Yes, she was happier than she had ever been.

She carried a tray of fresh drinks to the living room in time to hear the question again, the same one that no doubt was first on the nation's mind. This time Nona asked it.

"Do you think it will take as long to defeat the Japanese?"

Audrey was ready with her hopeful answer, but Mrs. Bailey gave one that was unexpected.

"I got it on good word that it won't be long now and Japan is going to have to surrender."

"Good word?" Nona asked.

"If you know people who clean the right houses, you hear things," replied Mrs. Bailey. "People in government are talkin' about the end of the war. Nobody was sayin' anything like that 'til last month. Gotta be somethin' to that."

Mrs. Bailey's "good word" was in doubt. That much was obvious from the less than immediate, less than enthusiastic response.

"I sure hope that's true," Ruth replied. "It would sure save a lot of lives."

Chapter 34

A war nearing its end meant realistic hope for security, for the United States, for the world, and an end to worldwide loss of life. It meant an end to rationing, an end to personal and community sacrifice, but what it meant right now was an end to the amazing production that had made Audrey and everyone at the Willow Run plant so proud. A finished Liberator out the door every 55 minutes—25 bombers a day—had come to an end. The numbers were no longer necessary. On June 28 the last Liberator, number 8,685, rolled out through the giant door, with the name *Henry Ford*; it seemed fitting.

Audrey stood with her crew and hundreds of workers and executives to watch their last contribution roll into the sunlight. It was a magnificent war machine, carrying the pride of Willow Run.

"We did it, Jack," Audrey said. "All of us. We did it."

Jack nodded. "Those are our planes that won this war. And Mr. Ford knows it. He's takin' his name off that Lib, wants the workers to sign her nose—us," he said, adding a proud smile. "This is the best damn job I've ever had."

The best for so many. The only job for some. Audrey joined the cheering throng as the plane came to a stop. There was much to celebrate—the pride, the victory, her independence. Her own place in the world, she'd found that here. But maybe more importantly, the world had grown larger than her grief, and offered redemption. Yes, there was much to celebrate today. It was the tomorrows that had her worried.

The rumors circulating for months had finally been confirmed, the Willow Run plant was being sold to Kaiser-Frazer for mass automobile production. Also confirmed was the fate of thousands of jobs.

Ruth dished out the casserole she'd brought home from the restaurant and joined Audrey at the table.

"Was anyone on your crew spared?" Ruth asked.

"Jack and Bennie."

"Only the men."

Audrey took a sip of her coffee. "Uh, huh. But I wouldn't want either of them to lose a job. Jack has a family to take care of, and Bennie, he doesn't have a lot of options."

"Do you think they will keep any women?"

"Maybe in clerical. Returning soldiers will have first option on the rest."

"Is Nona going to be okay?"

"She's the one who encouraged me to buy more government bonds. She knew it was only a matter of time for her, so she's been putting money away. Nona wants to get into college, and if anyone can do it, she can." She waited for Ruth to look up. "It's June I worry about. Two kids and a husband MIA. If I were working, I'd help her."

"I know you would."

Audrey leaned back against her chair. "I've got no place to go tomorrow," she said, as if the realization had just taken on its full weight. "I got no place to go, nothing to do." No purpose, no mission, no way of making her own money. That it frightened her was unexpected. Independence had seeped into her cells, as much a part of her as the blood coursing through her veins. Or so it seemed. "I just realized something," she said, worry evident in her tone. "The war was our protection, women like me. War, Ruth. The world full of fear and bombs and death. That world needed us. We were *essential*, so that made it alright—for them to hire us, for us to take advantage of the chance. A chance I never would have had if the world hadn't exploded in war. There is something about that, that seems very wrong."

"We can't choose our chances," Ruth replied. "Just take hold of them when they're there. There's nothing wrong with that."

"I don't think I'll ever see a chance like that again. What am I going to do now?"

"What are *we* going to do?" Ruth asked. "For now, we have a place to live, we have a car, and we have my job. Waitressing will never make the money you were making, but it's acceptable and I can't imagine any soldier walking into The Bomber to take over my apron."

The corners of Audrey's mouth lifted slightly. Ruth left her chair, circled behind Audrey, and wrapped her arms around her shoulders. She kissed the smooth, warm skin of Audrey's neck. "I know you are worried," Ruth said softly. "But we are going to be fine."

"I do know one thing. I do not have the patience you have working with the public. Martin would have my apron the first time I *accidentally* threw my hip into the back of a rude customer's chair."

"So, you will get another job." Ruth replied. "And as for doing something important? Oh, we have plenty to do."

Chapter 35

FIRST ATOMIC BOMB DROPPED ON JAPAN;
MISSILE IS EQUAL TO 20,000 TONS OF TNT;
TRUMAN WARNS FOE OF 'RAIN OF RUIN'
The New York Times, Tuesday, August 7, 1945

Japan had rejected the July 26th Big Three Ultimatum. So, carried in the belly of a special B-29, a uranium atomic bomb was dropped on the city of Hiroshima. The enemy was stunned, the destruction unprecedented. More deaths than any single bomb had ever caused, but still Japan rejected surrender. Three days after the first, a B-29 named Bockscar dropped another—a bigger, more powerful plutonium bomb, on the vital port of Nagasaki. Truman's warning of a "rain of ruin" was no bluff.

Just over a week later, with the anticipation of yet another bomb needed, Jack met Audrey at The Bomber where she had claimed a table for them in Ruth's section.

"How's the training going?" she asked as he eased into the chair across from her.

There was none of the usual urgency in his movements, no no-nonsense tone in his voice. "Ah, they act like I've never even seen the working end of a screwdriver. I could work any part of their assembly in my sleep. And so could you."

"I'm afraid I'll never get that chance again."

Jack slowly shook his head. "I know our boys need jobs when they come home, but it doesn't seem right to throw out an already trained work force."

"I wish the powers that be felt the same way," she replied. "I know there are a lot of women who are happy not to have to work now, but there are a lot of us who want and need to work, too."

"If it was up to me—"

But Martin burst from behind the counter. "It's over!" he shouted. "It's finally over! Japan has surrendered! NBC just announced it."

The restaurant erupted into shouts and cheers. Many stood, grabbing each other in celebratory embraces, and Audrey, too, stood and welcomed Jack's strong embrace.

"There it is," he said, before releasing her. "What we worked all those hours for."

Ruth squeezed between people and tables and made her way into Audrey's arms, and then Jack's. "It is really over, isn't it?" she said, her eyes wide, her face illuminated with excitement. "Things are going to be so much better, I just know it."

∽ ∽ ∽

Over? In the larger sense, yes, it was over. Life on the home front would be better in many ways. Remote pockets of enemy resistance in places like China, Guadalcanal, Peleliu, and parts of the Philippines would require continued military effort, and troops would be needed for the occupation, but today marked victory.

The trickle of returning soldiers would soon become a flow, the production of war machines and materials would drop to an all-time low, and society would be looking forward to returning to life as they knew it before the war.

It seemed the night should be a big night of celebration, and it did start out that way. It began with Jack and Lucy and the crew—everyone except June. The end of the war for her did not bring the joy that it brought the others. She had no husband coming home to celebrate, and still no word of either hope or closure. They would have to celebrate without her. A few drinks had turned to a bit of dancing, then morphed into a quieter night at Nona's.

Mrs. Bailey was attending a prayer celebration at the church, and Nona had begged off to spend the evening with Audrey and Ruth. Adding a few more drinks to the beers of earlier in the evening was all that Audrey needed to let emotion have full rein.

"It's not all good news, you know." She held her drink with both hands, leaned forward from her chair to rest her arms on her knees. "Not for us." She looked from Ruth to Nona sitting across from her on the davenport. "What are we going to do now?"

"I wish you wouldn't worry so much," Ruth replied. "We're going to be all right."

"How can you be so optimistic?" Audrey's frown lines deepened. "We've proven what we can do. We can do any job a man can do, as well as a man can do it—sometimes even better. But it's not going to matter, not anymore."

"Why are you so sure of that?" Ruth asked. "Just because you don't have the plant job doesn't mean there won't be something else."

"Then you haven't heard the same talk that I have. You've heard it, haven't you, Nona?"

"All my life." Her tone lacked the angry edge of Audrey's. " 'That's not your place', 'Who do you think you are?', 'You're just a Negro, you need to know your place.' And if it wasn't for my parents, I would have believed it."

"Not believing those limitations yourself is one thing, but if enough of the world believes them then you're trying to live in an echo chamber."

Ruth met Audrey's eyes. "You're admitting defeat before you've fully entered the war." Then Nona's eyes. "Are you surrendering, too, Nona?"

"Those limitations are just substitutions for the shackles we've already shed," Nona replied. "How could I justify negating the tenacity of Mary Terrell or the courage of Harriet Tubman? I have far fewer obstacles than they faced and look what they accomplished." She shook her head. "No, no surrender here. I'm stronger than I look, smarter than most will give me credit for, and I have a plan."

Ruth directed her words at Audrey. "You're right, we have proven a lot of things—to ourselves and to others. We've made a difference and we can continue to make a difference."

"I really believe," Nona said, "that anything is possible if we are willing to take the risks and if we can brave the bumps and bruises. Think about how you got the right to vote."

Audrey sat back in her chair. Her shoulders relaxed, her expression softened. "I know you're right, both of you. Neither of you let anger keep you from moving on." She nodded her resolve. "I have to learn to do that."

Chapter 36

Although a state of war still exists, it is at this time possible to declare, and I find it to be in the public interest to declare, that hostilities have terminated. Now, therefore, I, Harry S. Truman, President of the United States of America, do hereby proclaim the cessation of hostilities of World War II, effective twelve o'clock noon, December 31, 1945.

Doubt had made its way past confidence, slipped by expectation. It had taken nearly a year, but doubt had won its place in Audrey's life. It boasted after months of Audrey attempting to be a secretary, enduring a skirt and hose and condescending comments, unable to tame Remington keys that had a mind of their own. And it gloated now every morning as she cinched the wide belt tightly around the waist of the floral-printed tea dress, the required attire behind the J.L. Hudson jewelry counter.

Every time a job opportunity that she felt better suited for was filled by a man instead, Audrey lost hope that there would ever be another. And this job did nothing to change that.

She stared into the bathroom mirror at the reflection she refused to own. She smoothed the rouge over her cheeks and blotted her lipstick on a square of toilet paper. "You know," she said to Ruth peering over her shoulder and pinning up her hair, "if I added some white face paint around my eyes and mouth, I could join the circus."

"Don't say that, honey." Ruth slid her arms around Audrey's waist and kissed the tender skin below her ear. "You're beautiful, with or without makeup, in factory coveralls or a tea dress."

"You are sweet," she said with a grateful smile, "and biased. And I just hate that being acceptable means that I can't be me." Except here

211

in Ruth's arms, in Ruth's love—the one place on this earth where stripped naked to the bones of her soul didn't make her vulnerable, didn't put her at risk. She covered Ruth's arms with her own and turned her head to accept kisses to her cheek. "Without you," Audrey said, closing her eyes and letting love wrap her safely and making everything worth the charade, "I *would* have to run off to the circus."

"If it ever gets that bad, honey," Ruth whispered against Audrey's ear, "you'll be taking me with you."

∽ ∽ ∽

It wasn't the drive to Detroit that bothered Audrey. Looking beyond the limited job opportunities in Ypsilanti was a given. Compared to a job that had become a personal mission, though, selling jewelry seemed less than essential. And the wage, at a third of what she had made at Willow Run, was insulting. Insulting to her, to any woman, making her own way in the world. Disposable jobs and non-living wages sent a strong message—go back home or get married. Neither of which Audrey had any intention of doing.

But it was becoming more difficult by the day to keep the positives front and center in her thoughts. Temptation increased to say what for her own dignity needed to be said, and to demand the respect not only for herself but for the women she worked with.

Audrey placed her purse on the shelf of her locker in the break room and greeted her coworker. "Morning, Alice. Ready for another fun day in the Hudson glitz department?"

"Well, I am," she replied, missing the sarcasm altogether. "We have a new necklace and earring ensemble in today, silver and mother-of-pearl." She preened in the mirror on her locker door, repositioned a bobby pin, and reapplied ruby-red lipstick. "Remember," she added, "you can set aside a set and put it on account." She shut the locker door and smiled. "One of our Hudson perks."

Not a hint of sarcasm in Alice's voice. A little spending cash, the newest jewelry, a company payment plan, all perks Audrey understood that someone like Alice would appreciate. And that was okay—her husband was older and committed to his business, no time for a family yet. Alice was bored, and a tad unappreciated. Enough so that she was far more tolerant of the job and their department manager, Raymond Roth, than Audrey was.

Alice was busy examining the new ensemble and placing the display set in the glass case while Audrey began counting out the starting cash in the register drawer. But before she could finish she felt a hand on her waist and the brush of his body against her that always followed. Every muscle in her body tightened automatically. She clenched the muscles of her jaw to keep from saying what she so badly wanted to say.

Mr. Roth leaned forward over Audrey's shoulder, both hands now on her waist. "You need to smile more, Audrey. I want those sales numbers up today." He reached forward and lifted her hand. "I'll finish the count while you go back to the break room and put a fresh coat of polish on those nails."

Audrey turned to squeeze from the press of his body and he placed his hand over her buttock before she could get clear. Anger quickly shot past discomfort. Normally she made it to the end of the day, tolerating his liberties, suppressing the anger until she could dissipate it on the drive home. But this day had just begun.

She took as long as she dared, even after the polish dried, and then spent the rest of the morning strategically trying to keep a comfortable distance from Mr. Roth. The most effective strategy was to keep Alice physically between them, but that made her feel horrible each time Alice had to endure the wandering hands.

The bathroom had become Audrey's refuge for the first fifteen minutes of their lunch break. By that time the break room was full with everyone eating, talking, filling spaces. She could slip in, eat her sandwich, and allow the room to empty naturally. Today Alice took the last few minutes to go to her locker and Audrey took the opportunity to start the needed conversation.

"How do you keep your composure, Alice? I swear if he puts his hands on me one more time today I'm afraid I will be nowhere near polite."

"Oh, it's nothing, Audrey. Why would you fret over that? You're just upset over nothing."

"It doesn't bother you?"

"Oh, goodness no. A little attention's good for a woman's soul." Alice closed her locker, offered a wink and a smile, and sashayed from the room.

Is that what it was supposed to be, attention for a woman's soul? Maybe for Alice, maybe for some others, but nothing about *this* attention, *his* attention, felt right to Audrey. It should be *her* choice, shouldn't it, when and if it was okay? Or, was it her difference, her love for women that tainted it, made what was acceptable to others not acceptable to her? Alice *would* think it strange then, rejecting something so natural, so welcomed by *normal* women.

Audrey glanced at the two women who worked the men's jewelry counter as she crossed behind them to the women's counter. She'd watched them more closely over the past few days, wondering—what they thought, how they felt. Was it appreciation she had seen when his hands wandered and she saw nothing that had invited it, encouraged it? When they said nothing, was their silence permission? No words needed to accept the expected? Was that what she had seen?

No, she was sure of what she had seen—subtle flinches, averted eyes, and that quick little avoidance step she knew so well. Liberties unchallenged but not welcomed. She knew so little about these women, why they wanted to work, or needed to work. But regardless of why, they were here and she doubted that it was for "attention for their souls."

They were tolerating, as she was, saying nothing that might jeopardize their job, their independence. Need outweighing compromise. So, silence. All of them, for whatever their reasons. The only question left was for how long.

Chapter 37

April 1946

There was a change to the town these days. The air was clear of the smell of jet fuel, and strangely mute in the absence of the sound of planes, flying day and night. The sweet smell of summer honeysuckle floated free of the blanket of fuel fumes. Evidence of a pig roast in the park carried to the middle of town, along with children's laughter and excitement no longer drowned out by the drone of bomber engines. But The Bomber restaurant had changed very little—a few empty tables when before it had been filled to capacity, and menu items that had earlier been rationed, but little else. The walls were still covered with photos of Liberators, along with those of the plant, the crews, and the pilots who had proudly flown them. There was just one addition. Ruth's drawing of FDR, head tilted pensively, hung prominently on the wall behind the cash register.

It was home, this place, as much as her apartment, as much as her job had been. Audrey settled at a table next to the wall to wait. Good news brightened the smile she sent Ruth, waiting the last of her tables to finish her shift. And home, where her heart settled, was in the soul and the heart of the woman returning her smile.

Minutes later Ruth dropped into the chair across the table and released a sigh. "Done for the day. Done with new customer questions and demands. Done with being bumped with a tray of hot soup on board, and done with lousy tips." She offered Audrey a tired grin. "Tell me something good."

Audrey leaned forward and rested her elbows on the table. "I'll tell you two things. No, three. Good things should come in threes, I think." She acknowledged Ruth's lightened expression. "I'm done with

215

Mr. Fast Hands. I told him that women employees were there to earn a paycheck to pay their bills, they were not there to satisfy his cheap pleasures."

"That *is* good," Ruth replied. "I hated knowing that you put up with that every day. Do you think he will stop?"

"With me, yes. He fired me."

"Oh, no."

"Yes," Audrey said. "It's the second good thing."

"Well, then, the third better be a doozie."

"It is," she said, her voice lifting with excitement. "I have a new job, a real job."

"That fast? I can't believe it. I mean, of course I believe it, but wow. That's wonderful. What is it?"

"I'm going to be a driver. Part of me doesn't believe it myself. I was driving home after getting fired, and there was this delivery truck pulled off on the side of the road. I slowed way down when I saw this man kickin' the heck out of the front fender where the tire was as flat as this tabletop. I stopped and asked if he needed a ride and, you know, I think he was so frustrated that he didn't care if it was a woman or a beagle offering the ride. He was delivering ignition parts to the Willow Run plant, and all it took was me asking if they would fit in the car."

"So you helped him deliver them."

Audrey nodded. "It was so strange seeing cars being assembled there instead of our Libs. It just didn't seem right. But that was one grateful man. He owns the shop that makes those parts and he sure didn't want to lose that contract. He's expanding as fast as he can and he needs drivers."

"And something put you right where you needed to be, right when you needed to be there. Sometimes I wonder how that happens, but since I can't answer with anything rational, it becomes the luck of it." Ruth leaned forward, absorbed in thought. "But you know, I think it may be more than that. Maybe what we give out to the world comes back. What if you had driven on by and just thought, *That's an angry, frustrated man, and I'm glad I'm not in his place?*"

"He wouldn't have had the opportunity to offer me a job."

"And even though it wasn't your purpose in helping him, the result was a job."

"I wish I could believe that it always works that way."

"You have good reason to be skeptical," Ruth said. "I suppose we both do. Maybe there's no absolute. But isn't it a better hope to live by? Shouldn't we be putting our best out into the world anyway? We *have* seen it. Look at Nona."

"I couldn't understand how she kept offering kindness and forgiveness to such an ugly world. I don't think I could stand it myself," Audrey admitted. "But you're right. She was able to have a really good job and earned enough money to stick to her plan. Even with the servicemen filling admissions to the college, she kept reapplying until she got in."

"She has the patience of Job." Ruth smiled. " And she's going to make a fine teacher."

"I have no doubt of that. She's exactly where she's supposed to be." Audrey scanned the wall of pictures that documented an important part of her life. "I wonder," she said, her eyes returning to Ruth's, "if we will always be where we're supposed to be?"

"Let's just keep putting out there what we want to come back."

There was one thing she was sure of, Audrey thought as they left the restaurant, she was supposed to be wherever Ruth was. It wouldn't matter where they lived or where they worked, as long as they were together.

Ruth settled behind the wheel of the car. "I do know where we need to be tomorrow," she said, starting the engine.

"The woman Lillian called about last night?"

"Yes, and it's not going to be easy."

"I don't expect any of them to be easy."

Ruth continued as she pulled from the parking lot. "Well, this woman wants to keep her baby despite every known odd being against her. She has no place to live, no money, a newborn, and if that's not enough of a challenge, the baby's father is a wealthy, married politician."

"Let me guess," Audrey replied. "He wants no bastard heir showing up."

"Well, *no*. How inconvenient for him."

Audrey cocked her head and narrowed her eyes. "Let's see how inconvenient we can make it. Who says it's not up to her?" As the car headed left toward the west end of town, she added, "Where are we going, by the way?"

"Molly and I," Ruth patted the dash of her beloved car, "are taking you for a ride in the country."

Ruth naming the car still made Audrey smile. And her reasoning made good sense. Anything that important to their independence, that essential to their mission, deserved the dignity of a name. So Molly it would be.

Molly carried them comfortably out of the city and into the now familiar countryside. Much needed getaways from work and worry often included long leisurely rides, sandwiches for dinner, and stolen moments of affection in the open air. Today, Audrey assumed, would be a getaway that would serve to make devising a complicated mission plan a little more comfortable. Until, that is, Ruth pulled Molly into the drive of a neglected farmhouse set back a good distance from the road. It was apparent even from the road that the building had seen its best days long ago. The once straight porch roof now had a sway like the back of an old horse. There were broken windows, missing porch rails, and only sparse evidence of whitewash on the old board siding.

They continued up the drive and Audrey sent a questioning look at Ruth. "If I didn't know better," she said with another look at the house, "I'd say the war had come to the home front."

"And I say it's time for us to take another look at our finances."

"Our *finances*?"

Ruth smiled and pointed to a small sign tacked to one of the porch posts that read, *For Sale*.

"You cannot be serious," Audrey replied, as Ruth parked at the end of the drive and jumped out of the car.

"Come on," Ruth called, already making her way through the tall weeds toward the house.

Audrey followed, carefully stepped up the rotted steps to the porch and joined Ruth, who was peeking through the windows.

"It doesn't look as bad on the inside," Ruth said, her hands shading the glare on the glass. "The rooms on this floor are big, and it looks like the kitchen must be in the back. We could get the inside in shape first. I wonder how many bedrooms are upstairs."

"You *are* serious."

"Think about it," she said, excitedly grabbing Audrey's hand. "We have Molly, so we don't have to live in town. And it would make the perfect safe house whenever we need a temporary place for someone to stay. And I'll bet we can afford it now. What do you think?"

"I think you're crazy, and beautiful, and," she glanced around at the work that would be involved, "this is such a mess."

"But if I can handle a mixer . . ."

"Then why not a drill," Audrey replied with a wide grin.

"And a hammer—and a screwdriver—and whatever it takes."

"You think we could make it work, don't you?"

Ruth took Audrey's hands and squeezed them tightly. "If we go at it, I don't think there is anything we can't do."

"We're doing something important, aren't we?"

"We are, we absolutely are," Ruth replied.

The delight on Audrey's face had softened into pensiveness. "I wish . . ."

Ruth stroked the side of Audrey's face and stayed with her gaze, the eyes that often told her more than her words. "Velma," she said softly.

"I wish she could know the good that we have done, what more we want to do. I wish we could tell her our plans. Her heart would sing if she knew."

"Then we'll tell her, honey, " Ruth said. "You'll whisper it to the part of her that hears your voice, the part deep in her that feels your strength." She drew Audrey closer and there on the porch of their future, she kissed her. "She'll know all the important things," she whispered. "We'll always tell her."

Bywater
BOOKS

At Bywater Books we love good books about lesbians just like you do, and we're committed to bringing the best of contemporary lesbian writing to our avid readers. Our editorial team is dedicated to finding and developing outstanding writers who create books you won't want to put down.

We sponsor the Bywater Prize for Fiction to help with this quest. Each prizewinner receives $1,000 and publication of their novel. We have already discovered amazing writers like Jill Malone, Sally Bellerose, and Hilary Sloin through the Bywater Prize. Which exciting new writer will we find next?

For more information about Bywater Books and the annual Bywater Prize for Fiction, please visit our website.

www.bywaterbooks.com